PRAISE FOR CORINNA TURNER'S BOOKS

LIBERATION: nominated for the *Carnegie Medal Award 2016*
ELFLING: 1st prize, Teen Fiction, *CPA Book Awards 2019*
I AM MARGARET & *BANE'S EYES:* finalists, *CALA Award 2016/2018*
LIBERATION & *THE SIEGE OF REGINALD HILL:* 3rd place, *CPA Book Awards 2016/2019*

Corinna Turner was awarded the **St. Katherine Drexel Award** in **2022.**

PRAISE FOR *ELFLING*

I was instantly drawn in

EOIN COLFER, author of *Artemis Fowl* and former Childrens Laureate of Ireland

PRAISE FOR THE UNSPARKED SERIES

Beware: this series' vivid descriptions, heart-pounding drama, and fabulous characters are sure to lure you in, as well.

LESLEA WAHL, author of the Blindside series

A cross between Jurassic World *and* Mad Max*! Fun, fast paced. And sets up an incredible new world. I read it three times in two days!*

STEVEN R. MCEVOY, BookReviewsAndMore Blogger

Wow! So suspenseful you won't be able to put it down!

KATY HUTH JONES, author of *Treachery and Truth*

Jurassic Park *fans will love this!*

CAROLYN ASTFALK, author of *Rightfully Ours*

ALSO BY CORINNA TURNER:

I AM MARGARET series
For older teens and up

Brothers (*A Prequel Novella*)*
1: I Am Margaret*
1: Io Sono Margaret (Italian)
2: The Three Most Wanted*
3: Liberation*
4: Bane's Eyes*
5: Margo's Diary*
6: The Siege of Reginald Hill*
7: A Saint in the Family*
'The Underappreciated Virtues of Rusty Old Bicycles' *(Prequel short story) Also found in the anthology:* Secrets: Visible & Invisible*

I Am Margaret: The Play (*Adapted by Fiorella de Maria*)

UNSPARKED series
For tweens and up

Main Series:
1: Please Don't Feed the Dinosaurs
2: A Truly Raptor-ous Welcome*
3: PANIC!*
4: Farmgirls Die in Cages*
5: Wild Life*
6: A Right Rex Rodeo
7: FEAR
8: A Different Kind of Camouflage
9: A Different Kind of Freedom
10: What's Done is Done
11: Weigh the Odds†

Prequels:
BREACH!*
A Mom With Blue Feathers†
A Very Jurassic Christmas*

Short Stories (ebook only):
'Liam and the Hunters of Lee'Vi'
'A Truly Clawful Christmas'*
'A Very Jurassic Lent'
Also available as a paperback:
Three Clawsome Tales

FRIENDS IN HIGH PLACES series
For tweens and up

1: The Boy Who Knew (Carlo Acutis)*
2: Old Men Don't Walk to Egypt (Saint Joseph)*
3: Child, Unwanted (Margaret of Castello)*
4: A Lion for a Tomb (Ignatius of Antioch)

Do Carpenter's Dream of Wooden Sheep? (*Spin-off, comes between 1 & 2*)

1: El Chico Que Lo Sabia (Spanish)
1: Il Ragazzo Che Sapeva (Italian)

YESTERDAY & TOMORROW series
For adults and mature teens only
Someday: A Novella*
Eines Tages (German)
1: Tomorrow's Dead†

OTHER WORKS

For teens and up
Elfling*
'The Most Expensive Alley Cat in London' (Elfling *prequel short story*)

For tweens and up
Mandy Lamb & The Full Moon*
The Wolf, The Lamb, and The Air Balloon (Mandy Lamb *novella*)

For adults and new adults
Three Last Things *or* The Hounding of Carl Jarrold, Soulless Assassin*
A Changing of the Guard*
The Raven & The Yew†

† Coming Soon
* Awarded the Catholic Writers Guild *Seal of Approval*

THREE CLAWSOME TALES

CORINNA TURNER

CONTENTS

A NOTE FROM THE AUTHOR

This short story came about when the son of one of my fans had to go into hospital over Christmas for an operation. Since, like his father, he is also a keen unSPARKed reader, to brighten up his hospital-bound holiday season I decided to have him star in an unSPARKed adventure. I leave you to guess which character he is!

LIAM AND THE HUNTERS OF LEE'VI

TIME: 59 YEARS BEFORE THE MAIN UNSPARKED SERIES.

"See anything, Tam?"

"Nah. These Utahraptors are ghosts, far as I can tell." I lower my binoculars for a moment, flexing my stiff shoulders.

"They ain't ghosts." Jace continues quartering his quadrant without pause. "Farmers don't pay good money to have ghosts culled. Keep looking. Remember, if we get them before the New Year round-up, there's a bonus."

Sighing, I raise my binos again. I've been zooming in and out for so long my finger is getting tired.

Out of the corner of my eye, I catch the movement as Jace elbows Marty sharply in the ribs. "Marty! Wake up or forfeit your share, you lazy—"

Marty raises his head with a grunt, fumbling with his binos. "Hey, the boy's right, Jace. These critters are keeping a real low profile."

"So we outwait them, thicko."

Marty sighs even louder than I did and claps the binos to his eyes. From what I've seen so far, he's the easiest going of the three. And Jace is the boss—owns a full half of the habitat vehicle whereas Marty and Roddy only own a quarter each—so he can be freer with the name-calling than the rest of us. A hundred times freer than me, who don't own nothing. I'm just the assistant. Still, I ain't complaining. I could be back with—

Movement... I spin the wheel of the binos quickly, tensing. Then sigh again. "Just deinons." The pair of tan and cream deinonychuses, standing barely as high as a short man, ain't what we're after.

"Should we try a new spot?" says Roddy.

"Let's give it a few more hours here." Jace carries on scanning as he speaks. "We're smack in the heart of their territory and we've been here long enough they'll be losing their caution even if they did notice us arrive. We move and we risk scaring them off and having to wait all over again."

"Do raptors scare off that easily?" I ask.

An ominous silence from Jace…

"That were a serious question!" I say quickly. "Do they?"

"Not if they can see tasty little people walking around, sure, no." Jace has decided to give me the benefit of the doubt. "But a large, strange-smelling vehicle? They're smart enough to be wary."

"And we want them all in our sights before we fire, remember," says Roddy. "Or we'll be chasing all over after the stragglers."

"I know *that*," I say indignantly.

"All right, city-born. Keep your wig on."

That only makes me throw him a glare. I can't help being city-born. Some hunters are way too proud of the fact that their grandparents didn't flee to the cities like most people did after the government declared the escaped 're-creations' uncontainable. He just ignores me, though. At sixteen, I'm very much the cub in this den.

I return my attention to my section of wilderness, out there beyond the turret windows. Snow blankets the ground. "At least they'll be easy to spot," I point out. Their grey feathers should show up well against the white, their colored ruffs even more so.

"If they ever show themselves at all," grumbles Marty, but he's diligently checking his quadrant now. Doesn't want to miss his share, especially not when there's a bonus in the offing. I'm excited about the bonus, too. As a mere assistant, I get a fixed wage instead of a percentage share—and bonus money for me is up to Jace. But he says it's Christmas week and I'm out here working the same as them, so this time, I'll get a fifth share. *If* we can catch the Utahraptors before the hill farmers head out to round up their wild-roaming stock in three days time.

I begin a new sweep—then swing the binos quickly as another movement catches my eye. Probably that pair of deinons again…yep, there they are, high-stepping eagerly through the snow, heads stretched out. Following some tempting scent. I scan ahead of them, looking for something moving…

There. What the—?

"Boy! There's a *boy!*"

"A *what?*"

"A boy! Three o'clock, six hundred feet, *look!*"

I dump the binos on the console ledge, fumbling for my rifle. By the time I've got it aimed, Marty's raised the windows and Jace is on our side of the turret, his own rifle pointing the right way, though he immediately drops one hand to the Intercar button, flipping the loudspeaker switch.

The boy, slender and dark haired, is staggering through the snow as though he can barely walk, oblivious to the danger closing in from behind. As Jace's voice booms from the Habitat Vehicle's external speakers he stumbles, his head jerking up.

"Run, kid! There's a pair of carni'saurs on your tail!"

The boy stares around, his eyes darting over his shoulder, looking for the danger, then wildly scanning in our direction as he tries to spot us. With the hab'vi well muffled in camo netting and a layer of snow, it's no surprise we're invisible. I mean, that's the idea.

Jace's hand moves, swiping on the strobe light on top of the turret, sending eerie flickers dancing over the white landscape.

"Here! We've got you covered, but shift yourself!"

The boy lurches forward at a faster pace, but it's clear even the news about the two hungry carni'saurs isn't enough to get him running. But the deinons have slowed to a halt, peering towards the 'Vi. Or rather, the eye-searing light. Guess they don't know what it is and they're not sure they want to find out. With four crosshairs on them, they got that right.

"Get below and help him in, Tam," orders Jace. "He looks beat."

"Sure thing." I slide down the ladder into the Vi's main living area and move to the side door, pushing the button to make it slide back. Leaving my rifle just inside the door where I can grab it if I really need to, I drop down into the snow and go the last few steps to meet the boy. He's younger than me—several years younger. What the heck is he doing out here?

"Come on, it's okay." Catching his arm, I help him to the 'Vi and boost him up into it. With the huge ground clearance of a Hab'Vi, the floor level is higher than his head. Rolling up and in after him—I'm still a little too short for leaping in to be that easy—I hit the door close button and call up to the turret, "Clear."

The boy's lying on the floor, panting and shivering—cold or exertion or both. "Hey, you okay?" I help him sit up. "You're safe now. Relax."

"My family." His accent's strange, and he gasps the words, still panting hard. "We've got to get to my family!"

"Are they out there too?" My heart sinks.

The boy nods, flopping against the wall as though he can barely sit upright.

Jace's booted feet touch the floor with a soft thud. Roddy's already sliding down after him.

"His family are out there," I say urgently.

Jace swears, crouching beside the boy. "Hey, kid, whereabouts are your family? How far away?"

"I..." The boy struggles to keep his head up, his face drawn with exhaustion. "I've been walking since...since early this morning."

Early this morning? Aw, heck! It's two in the afternoon now.

Jace's face tightens into grim lines and Roddy winces. Jace scoops the kid up with a grunt of exertion—the boy ain't *that* young—and deposits him in the chair in front of the console. Swiping quickly at the screen, Jace brings up a map of the area, demanding, "Are they in a vehicle or on foot? Do you know where?"

"Vehicle," whispers the weary boy. "We were…we were driving along the minor road… the snow slipped… swept us off the road, down a hillside. My parents were unconscious…" He leans forward, his eyes frantically searching the map, dazed with fatigue, "my sisters, they were okay, but Abby had banged her knee… So…I came alone to find help…trying to cut across…reach the main highway…"

"Never mind that now." Jace's voice is soft. Soothing. "Just concentrate on the map. Where are they?"

The boy puts a hand on either side of the screen, staring down at it. Finally, after what seems like forever, his gaze firms and his finger moves to point at a small road ten miles to the north. "There. That was the road."

"Certain?"

"Yeah. I was reading the map for Dad. We were on that road when the avalanche happened."

"Okay." Jace turns his head to say, "Roddy, get us moving. Marty, back up the turret and keep a look-out. We need to move fast. Tam, get some hot food and drink for…what's your name, kid?"

The boy's head is drooping towards his chest, but he raises it again. "Liam. Liam McEvoy."

"Get some food for Liam. My name's Jace, Jace Lee, and this is the Lee'Vi. That's Marty gone up the turret and Roddy in the cab, my co-owners, and this cub's Tam, our assistant."

I'm not sure if Liam hears the introductions. "Will we be in time?" On his face, dread wars with painful hope.

"We'll get there as fast as we can, and you got here as fast as you could, clear enough, so there ain't nothing more that can be done."

Small comfort, if it ain't enough, but what can he say?

"Tam, soon as Liam's had something to eat and drink, get him in a sleeping bag to warm up and catch some Zs." He jabs a finger over his shoulder.

"What?" Liam struggles to sit up straight. "No, I can't sleep. My family—"

"When we reach the road, we're gonna need you rested and alert so you can tell us where it happened. We don't wanna drive right past. So for your family's sake, you need to rest while you can. Understood?"

Liam nods uncertainly. Jace probably seems alarmingly rough-spoken and abrupt. I remember when I first went to live with Uncle Mike, I thought he was angry every time he said anything, until I learned that hunters just don't mince their words the way city-folk do.

I start to make oatmeal on the stovetop, staggering now and then as the vehicle lurches and slides through the snow. Oatmeal's filling and quick. Jace makes a hot drink straight from the boiler tap, presses it into Liam's hands, and heads up the turret to join Marty. Coffee, but there's no chance it's going to keep Liam awake, in his condition. Soon I'm swapping the empty mug for a bowl of oatmeal.

"Here you go. Get that inside you."

Liam tucks in, his spoon moving in a rather stop-start manner as tiredness fights with hunger. But he soon pauses to look at me.

"Will we be in time?"

Aw, heck. "I, uh, I dunno. What sort of car was it? A city-car?" Not that raptors couldn't have peeled the stronger grilles off even a farm truck ten times over, by now. Grilles only provide good protection for a moving vehicle. And there's a pack of huge Utahraptors around here somewhere. Even bigger than a Dakotaraptor, taller than a tall man and many times longer. Unaccounted for.

Oh God, no. My stomach lurches. Is our missing quarry off devouring this boy's family? Is that why they haven't shown themselves around here? No, a Utahraptor pack's territory is huge, no reason it should be that.

Liam's nodding seriously in answer to my question. "We don't usually drive out-city much. We're on our way to spend New Year's Eve with our Uncle Greg. He moved to Exception State to take up an opportunity training thoroughbred dracorex for the racetrack there."

"Where are you coming from?" His accent ain't from around here, that's for sure.

"Kitchener, Ontario."

"Ontario? Where's that?"

He looks surprised. "Canada."

"Canada? Oh." That's like, a different *country*, right? "I dunno if I've ever met anyone from Canada."

"You have now. But it *was* a city-car. So, will we be in time?"

I spread my hands helplessly. "It's not really something I can predict. I mean, city-folk assume if you step foot outside your vehicle you'll be eaten on the spot, but that ain't true. I mean, if you pulled up somewhere quietly, especially in a 'Vi, without doing anything to attract attention, and you kept alert, you could take a walk and nine times out of ten, maybe even ninety-nine times out of a hundred, you'd get away with it. But the tenth—or hundredth—time you'd get eaten. And you get to ten—or even a hundred—very quick if you do it a lot, which is why hunters never ever go out-vehicle without cover.

"But, uh," reluctantly, I continue, "it's a fact that a broken down vehicle's more at risk. Even if a carni'saur doesn't know there may be people in it, it's still gonna attract attention. So if I said anything other than that *I don't know*, I'd be lying. But there's definitely a good chance. Especially if they just hunkered down and stayed quiet. The snow's probably hiding the car quite well. That's why we'll need you to point it out for us. So you'd better scoot up into that bedroom and get some sleep."

"It didn't look far on the map. Surely we'll be there ever so soon?"

I shake my head. "Nah, it's off-road all the way. Could be an hour or more, in these conditions. Get your head down. Actually, have another drink first. You must be dehydrated. Or did you eat some snow?"

He shakes his head. "I was too cold. And I couldn't think of anything but finding help."

I hand him a re-filled mug and he starts sipping immediately. It's cooling fast in the winter chill.

"Is one of those guys your dad?" he asks.

I shake my head. "Nah, my dad weren't much to write home about. Then he died when I were nine and my mum couldn't take me—or wouldn't. But her brother, my Uncle Mike, didn't think much of that, so he took me to live at his camp. He's a hunter. He taught me to shoot then started taking me out on hunting trips. I'm real grateful to him and all, but plain fact is we just don't get on and it were getting worse the older I got. So now I work for Jace and the Lee'Vi."

I do love Uncle Mike, so I prefer to tell it that way, clean and simple. Leaving out him drinking more and more until finally Jace found me hiding under the Lee'Vi that night in pouring rain and fetched me inside.

Liam stares at me. "How old are you?"

"Me? Sixteen. What about you?"

"Thirteen next week. But how can you work for Jace if you aren't an adult yet?"

I snort. "I am too an adult. I don't need no stupid number to make me a man."

"But is it legal?"

"If Uncle Mike says I can work for Jace, it is. And he fixed it up." Kinda. Jace got the whole story out'a me and in the morning he had a massive row with Uncle Mike, and it all ended with Uncle Mike letting Jace keep me, thank God. Jace didn't really need an assistant, so I try extra-hard to pull my weight.

"Oh."

Liam's mug's empty again. I touch his coat. "That's all wet. Take it off. I'll hang it up to dry." I move to the over-cab berth Jace waved at and reach up to open the door. "Scoot up into there, tuck yourself into that sleeping bag and get some rest."

Liam shrugs off the coat and gets to his feet, staggering as he crosses the tilting floor. The pizza image on his t-shirt makes my mouth water, but I've a feeling we won't be eating dinner any time soon.

"Oh, boots off too," I add.

He sinks down on the floor to unlace his sneakers and remove them, revealing socks with a vaguely familiar symbol patterning them. Then it clicks.

"Oh, Star…er…Trek. I used to watch that when I lived in-city. What a classic show, huh?"

Liam shoots me a startled look, but for the first time a smile spreads over his face. "I didn't know hunters liked things like that!"

I shrug, pleased to see him smile but embarrassed at having shown such interest. "We can only watch what we can get in old hard copy, in a camp. The net connection being so infrequent out in the wilds. But, sure."

He shoots a look up at the open doorway, only three foot high. "Is this your bunk?"

"My bunk? This, my friend, is the master bedroom. Jace's berth. The top cupboard bunk's mine." I point to an even smaller berth high up under the ceiling, over the kitchen area. "Marty and Roddy flip for the cab bedroom every year, apparently. Marty lost, last time. He's below me, though hoping for better after New Year's Day, if his luck's in. Go on, get warm and rested. The light control is by the door."

Liam climbs wearily up and crawls into the berth. I draw the door shut behind him to give him privacy and darkness to sleep, but leave it open a crack, since everything's so unfamiliar, then climb up to join Jace and Marty in the turret.

"The kid asleep?" asks Jace.

"Well, he's in your berth. I don't reckon he'll keep his eyes open long."

"Good. He looked wiped out."

"I'm well impressed with him," says Marty. "Coming out here on his own for help. Too bad it's another fifteen miles to the highway."

"What else could he do?" I say. "Even if someone drove along that minor road, how would they spot a car buried in the snow?"

Jace snorts. "The fact him coming out here was likely the only chance any of them had of surviving was no guarantee he'd be brave enough to do it. Always a few bodies to be found in their cars every spring, to prove *that*."

"I guess. I mean, I totally agree that he's a plucky kid. If something's ate his folks, maybe we can keep him."

Jace and Marty burst out laughing.

"Heck, Tam, he's not some stray," says Jace. "He's a city-boy and he's got an uncle and who knows what else, you heard him. Why would he want to stay with us?"

My cheeks burning, I start scanning the landscape for threats. "I was just…oh, never mind." Just trying to make myself feel better, I guess. I can't stop thinking about that missing raptor pack. Without thinking, I snap, "Can't Roddy go any faster?"

Oops, back seat driving, Jace's favorite thing *ever*…

"When you own a share in a 'Vi, you can tell your co-owners how to drive. Until then" —I duck the token swipe he aims at my ear and study the snowy scene outside harder than ever—"tongue behind your teeth, cub."

"Sure. Sorry, Jace."

The 'Vi shifts, making us stagger and grab hold of what we can, then the vehicle's sliding sideways, starting to fishtail. But we come to rest gently against a boulder, Roddy shifts down, and away we go again. No sound from the master bedroom, Liam must be sound asleep.

Marty catches my eye. "And that," he murmurs, "is why Roddy can't go any faster."

My face on fire, I take up my watch again. Yeah, if we'd been going fast, that minor slide could've ended a whole lot differently. Keep your tongue behind your teeth, cub.

+

My brain's getting foggy from staring at empty whiteness, and the light's taking on a pre-twilight hue when Roddy's voice finally comes from the com-speaker. "We'll be turning onto the minor road in just a minute."

"Okay." Jace releases the com button and glances at me. "Get the kid up and ready."

"Sure." I slide down the ladder and knock gently on the door of the master bedroom. "Liam? We're nearly there."

He clambers down, bleary eyed but moving with more energy than when he climbed up. His coat's still damp, so I hand him my second best one, and my old boots for his feet, since the sneakers are sodden too. He follows me up the turret ladder eagerly, but fear flickers in his grey eyes as he begins to look around at the landscape. Afraid what he might see?

The road is a normal minor road, unmaintained by the government. Farmers have stuck snow poles in along the sides, though they get thinner in wilder areas. We're passing along a very pole-scarce stretch when Liam tenses, peering up at the crags to the north of the road.

"I recognize that rock! It's like a triceratops. I was just thinking that a moment before the snow—" He peers around frantically, then points. "There! See where the snow's poured down across the road and into the valley."

Jace presses the com-pad. "Roddy, we're here."

He directs Roddy to the best stopping place and we stare out in silence, our eyes darting over crags and boulders and the odd stunted tree. A bit too much cover out there for my liking. But no sign of danger. No sign of those Utahraptors.

"Come on, what are we waiting for!" Liam grabs my arm, pulling me towards the hatch. "Let's go!"

Jace gently but firmly detaches him and turns him to face the window again. "In the circumstances, we won't do the sort of check we would normally, but we're gonna watch for ten minutes, kid."

"If there is something lurking," I tell Liam, "feeding ourselves to it won't help your folks, will it?"

"But it's so cold out there…"

"We gotta wait. Just keep your eyes peeled and shout if you see anything move."

Liam's a restless presence beside me as we carefully quarter the area, but he does look diligently, for whatever his untrained city-gaze is worth. When Jace finally says, "Okay, Marty, stay here and cover us," Liam's down the ladder again like a squirrel, almost as fast as if he'd slid down like a hunter.

"You stay here with Marty," Jace tells him, arriving behind him.

"Are you going to tie me up? Because otherwise, I'm coming!"

Jace directs a measuring look at him. Liam straightens, staring back defiantly. Crunch time. If Jace decides he's a little kid, he'll probably shut him in the critter cage for his own good. But if he decides he's a man, or near enough…

"Okay, you're coming. But don't blame me if you see something you'll wish you hadn't." He glances up to the turret as Roddy joins us by the side door. "All clear, Marty?"

"Clear."

The door slides open. Jace and Roddy leap down, I drop down, and Liam scrambles down after me. Snow crunches under our boots as we cross the road, then we're wading up to our knees. We don't usually get as much snow as this, around here. But it gets shallower as we head down into the valley. This is the wind-scoured slope. Except the thick band of avalanche fall, just to our right. If it can be called an avalanche. It was only the accumulation from the crags on the other side of the road. But I guess if it's enough to sweep a car away, it's an avalanche, right, however small?

"This way!" Liam takes the lead. "It's almost at the bottom."

We're already out of Marty's sight. He can warn us on the porta-com if he sees anything but there are places critters could approach from that he wouldn't see. Gripping my rifle tightly in my gloved hands, I concentrate on Marty's blind spots. Along the valley in both directions... That lower ground, there…

We'll be at the car soon.

"*Mum! Da*—" Liam's shout smothers against Jace's glove as Jace claps a hand over his mouth.

"Quiet! Don't be a fool!"

Liam hurries on as soon as Jace releases him, but I can see his face going a deep red color. Guess Jace doesn't need to explain why staying quiet is a real good idea right now.

The path Liam forced through the avalanche earlier is still there, more or less, and we reach the car easily enough. Drifting snow's piled up over the window so I help Liam clear it while Jace and Roddy keep watch.

"I just climbed out the window earlier," Liam whispers, scrubbing at an icy spot with one hand and tapping softly with the other as he tries to peer in. "They can open it for us…" His lips twitch as though he's dying to shout again and only just restraining himself. No sign of an entry, no sign of blood. It's looking hopeful. But so sign of life, either. Have they frozen to death in there? Please, no.

Finally, the glass is clear. But snow covers the other windows and we can't see. I unhook the penlight from my belt and shine it in.

"What?" Liam stares, his fingers splayed against the glass, as I move the light from one seat to the next. "What the—?"

The car is empty.

"No! Nooo…"

"Shhhhh," I grip Liam's shoulder, trying to comfort him. "Calm down. There's no blood, nothing's broken. They left the car by their own choice. Someone must have found them, taken them to safety. Right, Jace?"

Jace has turned the watching over to Roddy, and is already inspecting the snow for tracks. He goes all the way back to the road, then returns, climbing onto the car to check if anyone has approached it from another side.

Finally, he answers my question. "Yes and no. Someone found them, but whether safety's what they're headed towards... Liam, come here, are these your father's footprints?"

A look of horror crosses Liam's face at this casual question, but he goes to Jace and peers gamely at the marks on the ground. "Uh, he was wearing newish outdoor shoes. And, uh, these look about the right size. I guess?"

Jace points to another set. "Those are a woman's. Your mother's, I presume. And one child, maybe a year or two older than you. A girl, I'd guess. Limping badly."

"Abby! What about Zoey? She's younger than me."

Jace shakes his head. "Nothing. She was probably being carried. So we know this. Your parents both came around and were able to walk—unsteadily, but walk—away from here, but they didn't leave by the road. This guy," he jabs his finger at one final set of prints, "who found them didn't come by car. He came from the crags across the road and he took them back the same way."

"Didn't come by car?" Roddy shoots him a look, momentarily distracted from his watch. "Who'd be out here on foot?"

Another refugee from a car wreck?

As I move up and down the track, trying to avoid stepping on the important tracks, I glimpse another print. "Jace!"

Jace hurries to look. "Yeah, I saw it already, never mind about that now." He shoots me a stern look and I realize he was keeping quiet on purpose, not wanting to scare Liam. I dunno about Liam, but *I'm* scared. I've been hunting long enough to recognize a Dakotaraptor print when I see one. And at least one Dakotaraptor has checked the car out since Liam trod this track through the snow.

"Tam, identify these for me." Jace is waving to the prints of the mystery man.

What, me? I step forward and look closely. "Uh, grown-up, man, I think, medium size. Very well worn-in outdoor boots. Like, really worn. Probably due changing."

"You're saying what the prints tell you. I said identify the owner."

What? How am I supposed to— Wait, almost worn-out boots, medium-sized man... I glance at the prints again. "Could be that Desmond guy we delivered those supplies to the other week. Your friend?"

Jace nods. "Yes."

"But his place is nowhere near here, is it?"

Jace winces. "To drive the 'Vi there, it's over fifteen miles. We can't get through that crag country." He waves towards the other side of the road. "But on foot, it's less than five miles. Des found them, and he's taking them home with him."

"But…five miles! In this? Why would he try to do that?"

"What else would he do? The car's probably out of fuel for the heater by now, or would be long before morning. No guarantee anyone will come along that road for days. Little likelihood Liam would find help or even survive, no matter how brave his attempt. Their best chance was to get to Des's place."

"So, are we gonna drive there or what?" Unease creeps up my spine as I watch Jace frowning around, from track to crags to setting sun.

"We'll never get there before dark. Des's out there with two injured adults, a lame teenager, and a small child. I'd say their situation is desperate. They might make it, but they might well not. I think we have to catch up to them on foot, just as fast as we can."

My stomach flips over. We're gonna get stranded out there in the dark, if we're not careful, *miles* from the

'Vi. But with Liam's wide, pleading eyes flicking from me to Jace, I can't bring myself to voice an objection.

Jace raises the porta-com to his mouth and presses the switch. "Marty, we've gotta go after them on foot. Through the crags to Des's place. Grab the first aid kit and emergency supplies. We're coming back up."

Abandoning the 'Vi here means a second dangerous journey back to it in the morning but we don't have a lot of choice. Four men with guns are enough to make a pack of raptors at least pause before attacking. Three, not so much.

We head briskly back up to the road.

"Kid, you'd better stay with the 'Vi."

For a second I think Jace is talking to me and I begin to bristle, my stomach lurching between relief and indignation—then I realize he's looking at Liam.

"No. I'm sorry, but I can't do that. They're my family." The kid speaks politely this time, very soft and firm.

Jace tramps in silence for a while, then raises the porta-com again. "Marty, get a rifle out for Liam. Something small." He lowers the unit again. "Ever fired a gun, kid?"

Liam swallows. Shakes his head. "I'm not bad at karate…"

Jace snorts, the tension on his face momentarily relaxing into humor. "You are, huh? Well, if Tam cheeses you off, you can kick him into next week, but the raptors won't care what you can do with your bare hands. You take the rifle. But you keep it over your shoulder unless I tell you to. No touching. Understood?"

Liam nods uncertainly. But as Jace reaches the 'Vi and leaps up into it to check the supplies Marty's put together, he drops back to walk beside me. "What's the point giving me a gun if I'm not allowed to even touch it?"

"Because raptors recognize guns, usually. Five men with five guns is better than five men with four guns. But we don't have time to give you a lesson on gun safety right now and we sure don't want you to shoot any of us by accident."

"Oh." Liam flushes slightly, but nods.

Jace leaps back out of the 'Vi as we approach and hands Liam a light rifle. "Safety catch—here. You take it off to fire. But you *don't* remove it, not unless I tell you to or there's a raptor about to bite your head off. Understood?"

Liam nods and slings the rifle over his shoulder briskly, as though keen to prove he's taking all these orders seriously and avoid Jace changing his mind about letting him come.

Marty whistles softly. "Tam." I turn around and he tosses a backpack at me—*oof!* No time to waste, though. I simply shrug into the straps and adjust the waistband. Survival blankets, medical supplies, emergency rations. This stuff could save our lives—or Liam's family's lives.

Liam watches Jace, Roddy, and Marty slipping into similar backpacks, then gives me an inquiring look. "Should I have one of those?"

I shake my head. "No. After the day you've had and the length of your legs, you'll hold your own if you can even keep up, especially carrying that." I jerk my head at the unfamiliar weight of the rifle.

Liam pulls a face, but doesn't argue. Sensible kid. He must still be beat.

Jace is shutting the 'Vi door. We're really gonna do this?

Apparently. Jace heads briskly for the crags, his rifle at the ready. He pauses to look back, pointing silently to Marty, then Liam, then me, then Roddy. Giving us the order of march. Liam opens his mouth, then closes it as he figures it out. Silently, we follow Jace in the order given.

The light is dropping. I want to believe it isn't, but it is. It's already gonna be gloomy in among the crags.

Yep. My back prickles as we reach the top of the slope and step into the shadows. The temperature plummets immediately now we're out of the sun. Jace is moving fast, without the long terrain inspections hunters usually make when travelling out'Vi and uncovered. This is dodgy as heck. Still, there are five of us. Could be worse.

"Why do we keep stopping?" whispers Liam, as we pause for another all-too-brief inspection of the ground ahead.

"Checking for danger. We're making real good time, you know."

"I just want to find them. In time."

We move on before I can reply.

About three miles go by in this start-stop pattern and fifty-five minutes on my watch then Jace halts again in a ravine cum valleylet. He frowns at the ground. Guess the tracks just got interesting. But he swings round to me and Liam and makes a drinking motion. Take a break. Okay.

I watch him prowling around as Liam and I sit down and drink some water. We can't eat anything; all the food is sealed in scent-proof packs, only to be cut open in an emergency. Marty and Roddy take it in turns to watch and take a sip from their own bottles.

Shoulders slumped tiredly, Liam sits staring up at the sky. Orange-pink sunset covers one half, darkness the other. Night is coming with terrifying speed and we're still two miles from the dubious safety of Desmond's place. Surely we'll catch up to them soon? If nothing eats them first.

But they're still ahead of us. Nothing's got them yet. Unless... I glance at Jace, who's still busy inspecting the ground. What happened here?

I guess Liam can sense my unease. "Do you pray?" he asks suddenly.

"Uh…yeah, sure I pray."

"Are you praying now?"

"Uh…no. Guess I should be. Know any good saints?"

Liam brightens, a hint of enthusiasm shining through his exhaustion. "I've been asking Saint Ignatius of Loyola to help me all day. Since he was a soldier and he had to march and fight and stuff. And Saint Maximilian Kolbe, too. Since he knew all about desperate hopeless situations that he was never going to survive."

"We're gonna survive." I speak very firmly. "But, uh, those sound like good saints. I'll ask them too."

But before I can speak to these likely helpers, Jace is beckoning us all close. He speaks very softly, pointing around the area.

"The adults were struggling, the teenager even more so. Des tucked them into that crack under that rock, piled all that cut greenery in front for scent camouflage, and went on alone. He came back with a sled and put the lady and the teenager on it—and pulled it himself, thank God. Can you imagine what Des might try to harness up to a— Anyway, the man followed, carrying the child. But they can't be far ahead of us."

"Did you know Des had a sled?" muttered Marty.

"He had *half* a sled, last time we were here," Roddy mutters back. "He was making one. Must've finished it."

"And thank God for that," said Jace, waving us into line again.

As we head on briskly, I keep my eyes peeled—but I ask Saint Iguanodon—no, that ain't right, is it? Saint Ig… Saint Ig… Oh, well, Saint Ig, anyway, for his help and prayers. Guess he knows who I mean. And Saint Max—I can't remember his full name either. I would ask Liam—but that would mean unnecessary noise.

Speaking of unnecessary noise—Liam's gasp sounds loud in the twilight quiet. I spin around. He's staring into the crags, fumbling his rifle off his shoulder and pointing it that way. We all bring our guns up to aim, all except Marty, who keeps facing the other way, as he should.

Jace darts to Liam's side. "What?"

"A raptor. I saw a raptor. I swear! Peeping out from behind those rocks up there. It was looking right at us!"

Jace exchanges looks with Roddy. "Just one?"

Liam nods. "Big—tall as you! Brown, I think. Dakotaraptor, right?"

Jace nods in return. "Sounds like. What color was the ruff? You know, the brightly colored feathers around the neck and head."

Color? What difference does that make?

Liam looks startled too. "Uh…purplish? But it's so dark, I'm not sure."

Purple's a common ruff color on velociraptors, not so common on Dakota.

Jace is nodding, though. "Okay, it's probably a loner. She's unlikely to attack us while it's light; she ain't that dim. Let's move."

She? How does he know it's a she? I remember the paw print I found. Has it followed us all the way from the car?

Jace steps closer to Liam and lowers his voice so only I hear. "Next time, remember to take off your safety catch."

He strides onwards. I'd bet Liam's blushing but with darkness settling like a cloak over the crags and the shadows creeping out to envelop us, we simply hurry on, our pauses growing shorter and shorter. Soon, Jace has to use a red light to check the tracks now and then. The last thing we want to do is switch on proper lights and attract attention. Better to keep our night vision and creep—grope, if necessary—quietly through the dark even if it takes a bit longer. Except there's that raptor out there, watching already. Waiting for it to be too dark for us to see her coming?

I shudder. But, are we…yes, the ground is starting to slope downwards. Dippy Desmond lives at the base of a range of crags, right? Maybe we're nearly there.

Jace hurries faster and faster, as the risk of blundering into something dangerous is increasingly outweighed by the threat of what we suspect lurks in the gathering night. The Dakotaraptor will probably try to snatch Liam—he's the smallest and most portable. She could be away with him in seconds. I should stand well clear of him to increase my own chances of survival—I'm the next smallest, after all. But I find myself keeping closer to him, my cold fingers tight and aching around my rifle. I won't let her snatch him if I can help it—or me. Roddy's closed up tight behind me, and Liam's keeping close to Marty and Jace.

No, we won't make it easy for her. If it is a 'her'. I still dunno how Jace is so sure of that.

We come out onto a gentler slope and round a high tower of rock, passing into a crag-ringed basin. I hear Roddy let out a soft sigh behind me. Relief? When I glance back I can make out his dim shape, following me, alive and well, so I guess it is.

We're walking towards the crags at the back of the dell. And…is it? Yes! The dark outline of a cave looms ahead. Even though dippy Desmond don't have a fence, relief still explodes inside me. We made it.

But did *they*?

Tension winds my nerves tighter and tighter as we approach. I see Jace's shadowy hand reach out and draw aside a curtain—light spills out. *Someone's* home, at least. Jace moves inside, making no move to lower his rifle—Desmond's cave is little better than any other large cave in terms of security. Still, it's light, and warm, and provides at least the illusion of safety, though an illusion like that can be dangerous.

I step through behind Liam, blinking in the brightness of a couple of solar-powered lanterns. There's Desmond, in his old jeans and a worn sweater. And behind him…

"Mum! Dad!" I glimpse a sturdy man with glasses and a woman with dark hair, then Liam dashes forward, obscuring my view.

Okay, the mom, the dad, check, check. Sisters? My searching gaze finds a sleeping bundle with a shock of brown hair sticking out—the little sister, clearly. An older girl lies on Desmond's make-shift bed with her legs propped up, something wrapped around one knee. A scarf full of snow, by the look of it.

Sisters, one, two, check, check. A knot of anxiety in my chest loosens. Liam's folks are okay. Now we only have to worry about surviving a night unSPARKed and out'Vi.

Only.

"Jace! Roddy, Marty… What are you guys doing here at this time?" Desmond has noticed the influx of people into his cave at last. He trails off, watching Liam and the couple hugging one another wildly. "Oh! Is this *Liam?* Oh, thank God! Oh, praise the Lord! You found him! He's safe! Oh, this is wonderful! I couldn't think what to do. Even thought about trying to get Beauty to find him. Only thing is, I wasn't too sure what she'd do if she *did*. Oh, thank God he's safe!"

"Safe, huh?" snorts Marty, looking around uneasily.

Jace glances at Roddy. "Roddy, take first watch. Tam, second. Marty, third, I'll go fourth."

Good, second watch means I've got time to sit down and eat and chill a while beforehand. Maybe even get a nap.

Desmond watches Roddy settle near the entrance, his rifle resting ready across his knees and shakes his head, smiling. "There's no need for that. Nothing will bother us."

"Nothing bothers *you*," says Jace. "We ain't you and we ain't taking the risk."

Liam bounces over to us, all his tiredness forgotten as he grabs Jace and me and tows us to the man and the woman. "Tam! Jace! Guys! These are my parents! Mum, Dad, these guys rescued me and looked after me and came to save you guys without a thought for their own safety!"

Oh, we thought about it. We just did it anyway 'cos I guess Desmond ain't the only crazy one around. But when someone's in trouble, you do what's gotta be done, unless it's pure suicide, that's the hunter way. So I just smile. The man stands unsteadily, reaches out and clasps my hand. Awkwardly, I shake. He grabs Jace's hand too.

"I'm Steven and this is Andrea." He has the same strange accent as Liam. "We can't thank you enough. We didn't know what to do about Liam. When we came to and he'd gone... Having to leave him… It's been like we were trapped in a nightmare."

"Thank you! There just aren't *words!*" Andrea also drags herself to her feet. She hugs me and kisses my cheeks, making heat rush to them. She does the same to Jace, who takes it in his stride and simply grins. Marty doesn't seem to mind, but Roddy waves her away when she turns in his direction, his eyes still fixed on the cave entrance.

"And that's Abby and that's Zoey," Liam's telling us, pointing.

Abby gives us a wan smile. Jace moves towards her, swinging his backpack off. "Let me take a look at that knee. I don't recollect Des keeps a great deal of medical supplies around. I guess angels tend to his cuts and bruises." The girl smiles uncertainly, like she's not sure if he's joking or not. No wonder, if she's just spent several hours with Desmond. He's an odd guy, but kinda holy—at least, Jace thinks so.

When Desmond waves us all towards seats around the table, Steven and Andrea settle back into theirs stiffly, clearly exhausted and probably suffering splitting headaches. They'll have mild concussions at best. They should be in the hospital.

"I'm just getting a meal together," Desmond tells us. "I'd only just started, so I can make extra for you guys. Settle down, take your coats off."

A fire crackles cheerfully near the table. The hood and the pipe carrying smoke away are the most technologically advanced things in sight, except for the com-unit in the corner. Desmond believes in living at one with God and nature and doesn't like technology. Apparently he only has the com-unit because his bishop insisted.

As we approach the table, Zoey wakes up, sees her brother and leaps up with an ear-splitting squeal of excitement. Jace glances over his shoulder from where he now crouches beside Abby's knee. "Quiet! For pity's sake! Could you sound any tastier?"

Liam shoots Jace a look just before Zoey hurtles into his arms. "Uh, yeah, shhhh, Zoey. We need to play at being mice, okay?"

"Why?"

"Just, er, because."

"Because if you don't, something will eat you," says Jace mercilessly.

Zoey's eyes widen. Her mouth snaps shut. That's better. I move towards the table, just as Roddy yells, "DES!"

Zoey looks behind me—and screams. Liam spins around—his eyes widen and he pushes his sister behind him, swinging the rifle from his shoulder. I turn, getting my own rifle pointed…

A Dakotaraptor stands in the doorway, taller than Roddy and many times longer, brown-feathered, her purple ruff clearly visible in the light. Teeth bared.

"*DES?*" yells Roddy, his rifle aimed.

"NO!" Desmond rushes forward and Jace shouts, "Hold your fire! You'll hit Des!"

I stand, fingers white around my gun, my safety catch off—and I'm pretty sure I heard the click of Liam taking his off, too. What are we waiting for? Is Jace gonna led the mad hermit get eaten?

But Jace is at my shoulder now, his own rifle trained on the threat. "Wait," he orders. "Let Des handle it, if he can."

Handle it? How? He hasn't even got a rifle.

But the crazy man is marching towards the raptor, wagging his finger as though at a naughty child. "*Beauty!* What are you doing here? You know you aren't welcome when I've got visitors. Go on. You're scaring everyone. Go away. Come back when I'm on my own."

He stops only feet from the vicious predator. She gives a demanding call that echoes off the cave walls, making me and Marty clutch our rifles even tighter, though Jace doesn't flinch.

"No, Beauty," says Desmond sternly. "No food. When have I ever given you food when I have visitors here? Never. Go away, go on." He points firmly at the entrance.

The she-raptor hisses, her ruff flaring angrily. Her eyes stab us with a fierce territorial stare. One massive killing claw taps impatiently against the floor.

"Oh-God-save-us, Jace, let me shoot," moans Marty.

"It's Des's place, Marty. Leave her to him."

"Go on, Beauty. You aren't driving out four hunters and you know it. Shoo. Go on." Stepping even closer, Des reaches out, places a hand on the leathery cheek and turns the raptor's head towards the doorway. He slaps his other hand down on her feathery neck in a friendly manner and gives her a shove. "Go. Shoo. I'll see you tomorrow."

A miracle happens then, before my eyes. The huge raptor allows the man-handling. And simply pushes through the flap and disappears into the night.

That man just shooed a raptor away.

The breath goes out of me in a huge sigh. I lower my rifle, my hands shaking. Marty and Jace do too, though Roddy only lowers his a little, back into his guard position. I turn to find Liam, pale-faced, doing the same. Jace takes a quick step to him, checking his safety catch. Clearly it's back on, because Jace grins and slaps him on the back approvingly. "We'll make a hunter out of you yet, kid."

"What the heck was that, Jace?" My voice comes out embarrassingly high and thin.

Jace turns to me, still grinning, clearly as relieved as any of us despite his cool while it was happening. "*That* was Des's favorite raptor. The fool found her with a broken leg years ago and splinted it, took care of her. Now she drops in on him from time to time. Hasn't eaten him yet, for a wonder. She was a pack matriarch, now with that dodgy leg she's a loner. Lurks in this little scrap of territory nothing else wants, eating whatever she can catch herself or beg from Des, who like the fool he is feeds her."

Des accepts this uncomplimentary account with a shrug and a smile. "Why shouldn't I feed her? She's my friend. I'm about to feed *you*."

Jace shakes his head and returns to Abby. Zoey begins to cry. Liam puts his arm around her and hustles her to her parents' embrace. But soon we're all sitting around the table, even Abby—well, all except Roddy—and tucking into massive plates of root vegetables and steaks that I'm pretty sure come from the edmontosaur haunch we dropped off here a week or two ago, now well-smoked.

Then Desmond is laying out clothes and blankets in piles on the floor, trying to make nine extra beds. We hunters of the Lee'Vi end up rolled in our survival blankets because there just ain't enough to go around. But there's a fire and a roof and a guard on the 'door' and our bellies are full, so it could be worse.

A lot worse.

+

I'm tired and stiff when I wake. Jace is on watch, and he has good news, delivered in an undertone since everyone else is still asleep and all those hungry carni'saurs are still out there. The com-unit got a satellite lock in the night and he put through a call to Highway Patrol on the McEvoys' behalf.

Highway Patrol arrives in a large off-road tow vehicle just as we're finishing breakfast. After assessing the family's medical condition—conclusion, not too dire—they decide to go via the car and make at least a quick attempt to recover it immediately. That's great news for us, since it means we can go with them and avoid that five-mile walk unSPARKed. Thanks, God. Thanks, Saint Ig and Saint Max.

I try to learn their real names from Liam as we drive. It's been fun having him around. Like having a younger brother. But before long we're back at the 'Vi. We provide cover while Highway Patrol get a long cable down to the battered car and haul it back up to the road, securing it to the back of the patrol vehicle— and then it's time to part company.

"Bye, Liam," I say. "I hope you get to your Uncle Greg's for New Year's Day."

"I think we will," grins Liam. "Maybe I'll ride a dracorex."

"A thoroughbred race'saur?" I snort. "Rather you than me. Unless you're some sort of crack rider?"

"Nah. Maybe I'll ride an old retired one."

"That's a better idea. Well, bye."

Marty and Roddy are still up in the turret, covering everyone as they move from vehicle to vehicle.

Jace claps Liam on the shoulder. "Well, I hope God carries on watching over you the way he did this last twenty-four hours. And if you ever need a job…" He winks.

Liam grins again, his cheeks going pink. "Thanks, you guys. Well, bye." His parents are already in the Highway Patrol vehicle, sitting nice and still and taking it easy the way the patrollers told them to.

"Bye, Liam." I roll up into the 'Vi and stand, then my hand darts out to stop Jace closing the door. "Hey, Liam!" I call.

About to climb into the patrol vehicle, he looks around.

"Live long and prosper!"

An even bigger smile splits his face. "Peace and long life!" he yells back, which some corner of my brain tells me is the correct response. "And…" he adds, "good hunting!"

Yep. We've still got a pack of Utahraptors to find.

"Good hunting, Liam!"

A NOTE FROM THE AUTHOR

I wrote 'A Truly Clawful Christmas' as a Christmas short story for my email subscribers in 2022. It is Father Ben's 'origin story' and I think it gives a really fun insight into his character.

A TRULY CLAWFUL CHRISTMAS

TIME: 16 YEARS BEFORE THE MAIN UNSPARKED SERIES.

"I do not have time for this!"

Whirling the steering wheel to the left, I pull up on the parking brake, spinning my car a neat one-eighty degrees to slide sideways into an under-sized space in front of the diocesan administrative headquarters. The pair of raptor killing claws hanging from the rear-view mirror tap sharply against the windshield as we jerk to a halt, but I ignore them and grab my satchel, unable to help another mutter of, "Nope, I *don't* have time for this."

I throw open the door and leap out, slamming it behind me and hurrying away from my lightning-yellow Fury S16. Not a stupid-money car, but a lot more under the hood than your average run-around, which is the way I like it.

"Ugh, Benedict!" An older priest, taller and broader and darker-skinned even than me, stands two cars along, clutching his chest. "I thought someone was about to crash!"

"Sorry, Patrick. It's only me."

"So I see!" he rumbles. "*Must* you drive like you're on a rally track?"

"No point wasting the space. And I'm running late." That's my excuse. That and my foul mood. I entered the priesthood to care for parishioners' souls but right now there are a few of mine whose bodies I could happily strangle.

"We're in time. Relax."

With effort, I slow my stride to match his, walking with him toward the building. No time or not, it's the quarterly city-deanery meeting with the bishop, and I have to be here. Never mind that if I can't find a few more volunteers for the Christmas Bazaar today, I'll just have to cancel it...

At the door, Tommy, my best friend from seminary, passes me, but he's heading the other way, back into the parking lot.

"Hi and bye, Ben," he says. "I've been pinged."

"Bye, Tommy." He's a hospital chaplain and the dying rarely adhere to the bishop's meeting schedule. I smother a twinge of envy at the thought of hospital ministry. So much more front-line. I want to care for people's souls, build them up spiritually, but it feels like all I do is wade through an unending bog of practical considerations. Maybe I *should* ask for a transfer to something less parish-based. I need to go on retreat and pray about it.

Usually, I enjoy hearing how things are going in other parishes. Today, as Bishop Dennis calls the meeting to order and we all settle around the long oval table, I just feel frustrated beyond belief. I need to be on the phone to parishioners, not sitting through this tedious meeting.

Everyone wants the bazaar, but no one is volunteering to make it happen, like with so many other things. And today, Harold Miller, who not once in the last three years has allowed me to forget for one second that traveling by bus to the Shrine of Our Lady of Speedy Succor—thus requiring the disastrous stop-over at Green Acres Resort—was *all my idea*, even had the gall to ask why I've never volunteered to organize another diocesan pilgrimage!

Hastily, I push this worst injustice of all from my mind. Cancelling the Christmas Bazaar won't be good for the parish finances. But I can't put off a decision any longer...

I'm absently drawing—or deeply scoring—a scowling Christmas-hat wearing car on my notepad, names and faces of possible volunteers running through my mind, when an odd, tense silence in the room snaps my attention outward. Why is everyone looking at me? At me or at their hands. No one is meeting the bishop's eyes.

I glance at Bishop Dennis. He's looking at me too. He was just speaking, right? What did I miss?

The silence draws on. Uh-oh, am I supposed to be replying to something? "Uh, excuse me, Your Excellency, could you repeat that?"

His lips tighten. Usually he takes nappers and doodlers in his stride with gentle humor, so he must be out of sorts today. "I was just talking about Father Gestadt."

Jerry Gestadt? He's one of the diocese's three rural priests, doomed to drive unSPARKed outside the city, month-in, month-out, taking his life in his hands on a daily basis to minister to the farmers—and even to the hunters—who live out there among the raptors and T. rex. I manage not to shudder, just. That pilgrimage stopover at Green Acres Resort was enough to confirm all my worst suspicions about country life. I don't envy poor Father Gestadt, that's for sure.

"Jerry?" I glance around the long table. No, he's not here. "Is he okay?"

"I was just saying that he has…well, no point beating around the bush. He's suffered a nervous breakdown. I've had to put him on immediate sabbatical. He's settling into a highly recommended clinic while we speak and they're optimistic he'll make a good recovery."

Everyone is still looking at me. "Uh…I'm sorry to hear that. Glad he's getting proper help."

I guess he finally saw one raptor too many, poor man. He always did seem something of a nervous wreck.

"Yes. Well, it's almost Christmas, he needs replacing immediately. Rural Catholics wait long enough for their Sacraments at this time of year. I've just asked for a volunteer."

A snort escapes me, and a few honest words. "Yeah? Good luck with *that.*"

The odd silence falls again. All along the table priests eye their styluses, their hand-pads, their pens, their notebooks, their fingernails—and shoot glances at me. My back prickles coldly. What?

"Uh…" Father Tredworth, a small, middle-aged, very pale-skinned man with unfortunately mouse-like manners, finally speaks. "Benedict, haven't you been, uh, raptor hunting?"

"Yes, you've got that terrifying necklace in your car," rumbles Father Patrick.

"Shot it yourself, I remember you telling me," murmurs thin, would-be-ascetic Father Wang, one of the city's few younger priests, eyeing me just a touch less calmly than usual. "Very proud of it, you seemed."

My mouth's gone so dry I have to moisten it twice before I can speak. "That…that was a freak accident! And…y'know, highly traumatic…"

"The counselor sent you packing after the third session," says Bishop Dennis, eyeing me over his spectacles. "*Should be traumatized but isn't*, that was her summary."

"I…I was highly…" I stop, swallowing. Was I? I don't have happy memories of the whole incident, but bar a once-in-a-blue-moon nightmare have I honestly had any very serious aftereffects? Except for a perfectly rational avoidance of out-city travel?

"I was just in the wrong place at the wrong time," I manage.

"From what I've read about that tragic breach in both your report and the media, you were very much in the right place at the right time. You saved that little girl's life and your calm assistance was a great benefit to the hunters as they dealt with the situation. And your successful rally-driving career before you entered seminary also proves you are good under pressure. To say nothing of your skill in off-road driving. And unSPARKed driving, at that."

"*UnSPARKed* driving?" I splutter. "Rally driving isn't unSPARKed! Most of the tracks have permanent fences and any that don't, Highway Patrol set up temporary fencing and they hire hunters to secure the sites. There's not a single race that's unSPARKed—

except the insane Hunter Open Rally and only hunters compete in *that*."

"Well, speaking of hunters, you visit the 'Vi-park quite regularly, I believe? Say Mass for the hunters, listen to their confessions… You're very popular with them, isn't that so?"

I swallow, and try to revert to a stronger argument. "I have never driven unSPARKed in my life!"

"But you have the off-road skills. You are obviously well-suited to tense situations and not easily fazed by, uh, dangers of a certain nature."

Wildlife, you mean.

He falls silent and just looks at me. Invitingly.

I've just asked for a volunteer. His words ring through my mind.

Everyone is staring at me now. I'm pierced by so many gazes, nervous, worried, pleading, feverishly hopeful… The older priests look less concerned, but everyone under fifty stares silently at the young priest with the claw necklace. Begging me to save them.

A rural priest? Me? That pilgrimage to the Shrine of Our Lady of Speedy Succor was the longest I've ever been properly out-city in my life—rally-tracks just *do not count*! This is ridiculous. Why *me*?

I look back at all the eyes, my mind rifling through names and bios, frantically searching for a more suitable candidate and coming up short.

They're all as city born and bred as I am. I was pleased when that claw necklace turned up in the mail, a few months after the Green Acres debacle—now I'm thinking Isaiah Wilson may have unwittingly done me a very bad turn indeed. No, I can't blame him. I didn't have to show it off as much as I did, hang it in pride of place in my car. *Don't you know pride comes before a fall, Ben?* I suppose my rally career would've made me a prime target anyway. Rural priests spend so much time driving on poor roads.

Finally, reluctantly, I risk a prayer. *Lord? I shouldn't offer, right? It can't be Your Will. I have so much to do in my parish. And I'm so unsuitable…*

I wait, hopefully, for some sense of confirmation, anything at all I can discern…but all that pops into my head is:

Someone has to do it.

The thought is so unwelcome, so intrusive, it could well be an Answer. I swallow.

Everyone stares at me, harder and harder, like they're willing me to speak. Cogs are turning behind some of those eyes, as they evolve stronger per-suasions, better arguments. The scapegoat has been picked, the sacrificial lamb chosen. Could I get out of it even if I tried? How undignified do I want to make this? Do I want to be a captain going down with his ship or a worm wriggling on a hook?

I meet Bishop Dennis's eyes. "Your Excellency, I'm willing to take on the role of rural priest, if you wish it."

An audible sigh goes around the table, the psychic wave of relief almost enough to knock me off my chair. Shoulders relax, faces smile, fingers ease their death grips on pens and styluses. It could be the Sistine Chapel after a new pope is chosen. Well, I've certainly made a lot of people happy with a very few words. The more they relax, the more my stomach clenches up. Did I really just…?

Bishop Dennis is beaming. "I do think you are far and away the stand-out candidate, Benedict, and I'm so glad you agree."

Low magnitude earth tremors shake my insides, now. "When…when would you like me to start?"

"Oh, immediately! Well, you will need a week, I'm sure, to tie up the bare essentials and get yourself organized. That will still get you out there in time for Christmas. I'll scare up a few retired priests to cover the Christmas services in your old parish, until I can appoint someone permanent."

A week? One week to downsize into a tiny living van and prepare for life on the road, surrounded by hungry carni'saurs?

"You will have a little suite at the Sanctuary House, of course, where you can leave some additional things," Bishop Dennis burbles on, seeming deliriously happy to have solved his most serious problem without having to hogtie someone and aim a fully loaded barrel of emotional blackmail at his head—or, heaven forbid, invoke Obedience. Did I surrender too easily?

Someone has to do it. Again the words pop into my head.

Guess not.

+

When the meeting breaks up, most of my brother priests sidle away from me with awkward smiles—or muttered good wishes for the future, hah! Father Wang offers clumsy congratulations on my new assignment as we move down the stairs and through the lobby. Only Father Patrick claps me on the shoulder and with almost hunter-like frankness, says, "Bad luck, Ben."

"Sorry, Benedict," mumbles Father Tredworth, scurrying past with his eyes cast down, wringing his pale hands as though unable to look at me.

"Ah, relax, Mouseworth," I call after him. "Someone else would've fired the first shot if you hadn't."

He shoots me a grateful smile and scampers away, bless him. He's an awfully sweet fellow, but not exactly rural priest material. He needn't have worried. Rural priest material? And who is rural priest material? Me? Hardly.

"You're the perfect choice," says old hunched-over Father Bruno, reaching up to grip my shoulder.

"Better suited than poor Jerry ever was." Father Pine, tall and thin as his namesake, nods firmly and heads for the door.

"See." Patrick buffets me with his arm. "*First shot,* eh? You know the right terminology already. You'll do fine."

I say nothing. Terminology won't save me from what's out there. I walk slowly back to my Fury S16 and sink into the driver's seat, feeling kinda detached from everything. Shock, I guess. I should grab a coffee at the first drive-thru and take a moment.

But when I close my hands around the steering wheel, something else hits me.

My *car.* I'll have to sell it. No point keeping it for the brief times I'll be in city. Total waste.

The anguish that stabs my chest is…mortifying. Guess I'm a little too fond of this car, huh?

Get a grip, Ben. It's just a thing.

I don't need to sell it this week, anyway. I'll have enough to do. And what if I'm totally useless at the job and the bishop reassigns me almost straight away?

Yeah, no point being too quick to ditch my Fury. I can park it at Sanctuary House to begin with. I won't worry about it for now.

+

Throwing the car keys on the hall table, I walk into the main room of my little presbytery apartment and look around at my clutter. Draw a deep breath. Run a hand through my tightly curling hair. Heck. Where do I even start? Talk about feeling overwhelmed.

One van. That's all the space I'll have from day-to-day. And not that large a van. I've seen the living vans in the diocesan parking lot now and then.

I can't even start, right now. I turn around and walk out again, heading into the church. I did stop for a coffee and I feel a bit less out of it, but…calm would not be the word. I kneel and close my eyes but my heart thumps too hard and my hands grip each other too tight. I need to face my fear head on.

Raptors. T. rex. All manner of carnivorous things with very big teeth and very sharp claws. Most a lot bigger and stronger than me.

Sure, I kept pretty calm at the Green Acres breach, but I got through that on pure adrenalin. When I was finally on that bus, safe, driving away, I went wobbly as a piece of jello. Shut myself in the bus toilet for half an hour and sobbed. Shaking. Just shaking to pieces. Adrenalin come-down. I was familiar enough with those from the rallying, but I'd never had one like *that*.

I can't get through the next…heck, how long will I be out there for? Jerry Gestadt's been a rural priest for years, but he was older than me when he was appointed…I think. I could be driving out there for *decades*. For the rest of my working life. I can't get through that on *adrenalin*.

How am I going to cope?

Lord? Why are you doing this to me? I can't prevent the whiney thought.

Someone has to do it.

Huh. Guess we're back to that again.

I just have to accept that since this morning my chances of prematurely ending my life torn to shreds, eaten, gone with nothing to bury, have risen steeply. My heart pounds harder as I struggle to think about things rationally. But...but on the other hand, my chances of being knocked down by traffic, killed in a mugging, or dead in some city-accident will also be correspondingly lower. So maybe, statistically, it's not even that bad.

I focus on the crucifix over the altar and a pang of guilt twists my gut. Being eaten's not that slow a way to go, compared to...

Sorry, Lord. I guess I shouldn't complain. It might not even happen.

+

It's the car that's preying on my mind when I wake in the morning, groggy after staying up far too late talking on the phone to Tommy and then failing to sleep for hours. The car or, rather, my reaction to the thought of losing it. I call the diocese to check when I can collect the van—tomorrow—then I take some photos of the Fury and list it for sale on the Net. If the rural priest thing doesn't work out, I can buy another car. Anyway, it would have to be going bad beyond bad for Bishop Dennis to reassign me. There being such an overflow of eager volunteers to take my place.

And if I could get eaten any time from now on, I need to take my spiritual life to the next level. So… *Bye-bye, car. I love you too much.*

Ignoring the accusing voice that tells me I could have been knocked down crossing the road or felled by a random disease at any time so shouldn't I have been working just as hard on my soul in-city—better late than never—I find a couple of cardboard boxes and start grabbing essentials from among my stuff, ready to put into the van. When I've got everything I actually need, I can just box most of the rest up to go to a thrift store.

Twinge.

Face it, Ben, most of it's junk anyway.

Yeah? But it's *my* junk.

Not for much longer.

+

"A baptism. That's the thing not to miss. On Saturday." Father Gestadt sits in a recliner chair in his clean, quiet clinic room, swathed in a cozy toweling robe, looking pale and insubstantial. The clinic staff said I could see him for a few minutes as long as I didn't upset him. "Well, it's a carol service too. But the bit you have to be there for is the baptism."

"Right. Well, they gave me your schedule, so that shouldn't be a problem."

"A little girl, born in the summer. Nice young family."

"In the summer?" My eyebrows go up. "I'd have thought rural families would baptize their kids quicker than that!" Oops, I'm not supposed to talk about dangerous things. Does that comment edge too close…?

Father Gestadt just smiles and shakes his head. "Oh, it's only a conditional baptism. Farmers and hunters baptize their kids near enough the moment they pop out of the birth canal, you can be sure. Then they get the priest to come and do it again, often as not, since the priest's 'supposed to do it' and they want to be sure."

My eyebrows go up. "But it's strongly discouraged to perform even a conditional baptism unless there is actual doubt."

Father Gestadt just shakes his head again. "Local custom, Ben, and local need. Bishop Dennis is okay with it. Just do the conditional baptisms. The only thing that happens if you try to refuse is that they stop admitting they've already done it. Which is even worse. Hunters are the worst. Suspicious lot."

"They've been friendly enough in the 'Vi-park."

Father Gestadt gives a quavery snort. "The 'Vi-park! Yes, indeed. Try getting into a camp and you'll see the difference. The one tip I can give you about hunter camps is: be careful about showing disapproval. If they think you're going to report them to the city authorities, cause trouble, they'll never ask you back. City authorities are only one degree more welcome than Satan himself, in a hunter camp. You really feel you need to criticize something, make sure you're practically one of the family before you try. And if you are invited to a camp, be discreet. Don't mention it to anyone who doesn't need to know. Hunters have this paranoid idea that city-authorities will lean on you if they know you visit them."

"I'll bear that in mind."

Hunters weren't something I'd been worrying about, but they are real rough, tough guys, and by all accounts the women aren't much better. The idea of going alone into a camp full of them…if they didn't welcome my presence…

"They won't *hurt* you, mind." Jerry clearly sees my unease. "Send you packing, but never hurt you. Not a priest."

Well, that's something.

"The other thing about rural folk," he continues, "hunters especially, is that they're really into Saint Desmond the Hermit. Understandable, but some of them take it to extremes. Try to be patient. Talking to

God via Saint Des is better than not talking to God at all."

"Right." I frown slightly. Veneration of Saint Desmond in the countryside is threatening to turn into a folk religion in its own right, from what I've heard. But Father Gestadt does have a point.

"He's the saint for you now, anyway," Father Gestadt adds, his voice shaking slightly. "I told them to leave the dash statue in the van for you. You'll…you'll be glad of it…"

Before I can ask if he means glad of it because it will help me fit in, or glad on a spiritual level, he abruptly burst into tears, muttering apologies through his sobs. My unsuccessful attempts to reassure him end when a nurse bustles in and chases me out.

"Good luck!" Father Gestadt's thin choked voice drifts after me. "God bless you, lad. I'm sorry…so sorry…"

+

I spin the wheel, aiming the truck between two little chalets. A glance in the mirror shows the T. rex following close behind. A shot from above and a raptor smashes down on the hood, making me jump, but I manage to keep the swerve to a minimum as the raptor topples off.

"Sorry!" Isaiah's voice comes from above the cab.

I grip the wheel tighter, trying to keep us on course, concentrating as hard on the driving as I can. But part of me is hyper-aware of the young hunter's legs beside me, waiting for them to suddenly disappear upward as something drags him out through the sun roof…but he just shifts a heavily booted foot, wedging himself more firmly, and fires again…

I jerk awake, coated in sweat, then groan, relaxing into the pillows. That's the third time I've dreamed about the breach tonight. Last night I simply couldn't sleep. Tonight I can't sleep without dreaming.

The glow from my bedside clock dimly illuminates my comfortable bedroom. Why did this have to happen? I don't want to go out there and be scared all the time. I don't want to end up eaten. Or like poor Jerry…

Someone has to do it.

Yeah? But why does it have to be me, Lord?

+

The young guy pulls out of the diocesan parking lot, beaming, his fingers wrapped firmly around the steering wheel of my pride and joy—his pride and joy, now. The first guy to come and view… Well, I did offer a good price.

Sighing, I wind the leather cord of my claw necklace around my hand, the claws cupped in my palm, slip my Marian visor shield safely into my pocket, and head inside.

"Hi, May," I greet the receptionist. "I'm here to pick up a van."

The way she stares at me, eyes wide and awe-filled, takes me aback, until I recognize the look. It's the way I used to look at Father Gestadt and the other two. The way most priests, diocesan workers, and laypeople look at rural priests. Embarrassing as heck since I haven't even driven out the city gates yet and I may be back a gibbering wreck in a day or two.

"Of course, Father Ben. Here are the keys. You probably saw it parked out front."

"Yeah. Do I need to sign anything?"

She slides a hand-pad over the desk. "Just here."

"Right." Trying not to feel like I'm signing my life away, I scrawl quickly and pick up the keys. "I'd better get off."

"You will be careful out there, won't you, Father?"

Sure, like I'm going to drive into a raptor nest for the heck of it. People do say the silliest things when they're trying to be nice. Still, it's nothing like as bad as what some of my parishioners have been saying since they found out. Harold Miller wanted me to sue the bishop for reckless endangerment.

"Sure will. Bye, May."

The van is painted black, of course, with a white dorsal stripe running up the middle of the front bumper, along the center of the roof and down the middle of the rear bumper, evoking a priest's collar. SOS vans, they're nick-named. As in, Save Our Souls.

Right now it feels like I need to work hardest on my own. Maybe that's nothing new, just something ignored.

Resisting the urge to unlock the back and take a good look around, I get into the driver's seat and put the key in the ignition. This is what I've got, and I'll have to make do with it. It's not a new van, but not a heap of scrap either.

The engine roars into life strongly enough, but my heart sinks as I remember the sweet purr of my Fury. Still, the van's got power, and it's got four-wheel drive. Could be worse.

It needs the power just to move itself, I realize, as I press the gas and pull out into the traffic. And I haven't loaded it up yet. Guess my days of showing off at the wheel are over.

+

When my parish—former parish—building comes into sight—church on the first floor, hall on the second, offices and meeting rooms above, mine-for-not-much-longer apartment at the top—Tommy's green Sierra is parked out front. He puts aside a hand-pad and gets out as I pull to a halt. No hand brake turns in this thing—it would probably end up on its back with all four wheels in the air.

"So, your new wheels, huh?" Tommy greets me. "Christmas present from the diocese."

"It's still Advent," I grumble. For another two weeks.

Tommy ignores my grumpiness. "Let's see, then."

I press the button to unlock the rear side door so he can open it, pushing aside the sliding panel to climb into the back direct from the driver's seat. Hunting around in the daylight from the door and the single side window, we find a control panel and get the interior lights on. It feels cramped even with just the two of us looming in the aisle. There's a bed, a kitchenette, a few cupboards—one of which turns out to be a minuscule shower and toilet—will I even fit in there?—and not a lot more.

"Well, it's a down-size, right enough," says Tommy. "But it's got everything you need."

"Except armor." The sour words slip out. A hunter's Hab'Vi, or Habitation Vehicle, will be sheathed in steel plates and external shutters. The cheapest might only be certified up to large raptor, but the vast majority will withstand anything up to and including an allosaur. Unlike this toy van.

Tommy laughs uneasily, busy looking in drawers. "You're not supposed to need it, are you? You'll always be parking at farms. Hey, here's a manual. *How to get the most out of your Roman 65 Living Van conversion.*" He holds up a dog-eared physical book. "Huh, this first line is in bold capitals: THIS IS NOT A HABITATION VEHICLE AND IS NOT SUITABLE FOR SLEEPING UNSPARKED."

"Like I said, no armor. It's just a sleep pod on wheels."

"Relax, Ben. You're going to do great."

"Why do people keep saying that?"

"Because it's true. If Bishop Dennis were a little pushier he should have retired Jerry long before this and given you the job. The poor guy was clearly in over his head and sinking fast. Hard to imagine he was ever well-suited to it."

"Yeah? How would we know? We were in grade school when he was appointed. Maybe he was the perfect candidate back then, and this is what the job does to you."

Ever since I saw Jerry yesterday I've been unable to shake off the little voice that keeps asking: Is that what I'm going to be like, in twenty, thirty years? Jumping at sudden movements? Bursting into tears at a mere thought?

Tommy reads my mind. "You're not Jerry, Ben. You'll be fine. The breach at the resort proves that."

"I got through that on *adrenalin*!" Only as my words echo back at me from the too-close walls do I realize I'm shouting. I lower my voice with effort. "Adrenalin, Tommy. After I had to go out after Mei Ling I was so high on the stuff I just followed the hunters' lead. And they were stark raving mad, I can tell you."

Again, I remember how Isaiah, little eighteen-year-old Isaiah, just whipped out his knife and gashed his arm open so he could play live bait to a Tyrannosaurus rex. Mad, both of them, and thank God for it, because they saved everyone who was left alive to save. The casual courage they displayed was quite something, but nothing I would normally expect to be able to imitate.

"I'm no braver than you or anyone else," I persist. "First hint of trouble and I may fall apart."

Tommy just smiles, shaking his head from side-to-side in a seriously annoying way. "I would never rally-drive, Ben, and nor would most people. Your only problem is lack of faith in yourself. Or excessive humility. I'm not sure which. Keep stressing if you insist. I think you're going to be a great rural priest. Haven't you been seriously discerning whether to apply for a change?"

"Hospital or prison ministry, maybe even an emergency services chaplain, not *this!*"

"Parish life doesn't suit you, Ben. It's slowly smothering you and you know it. You need a bit more adrenalin in your daily life, something more front line, hands on. Seems God's answered your prayer."

"Or called my number."

"Well, he is allowed to call your number, y'know," says Tommy ruthlessly. "But I doubt he has. He's just found you something that suits you better." He shoots me a look, a teasing smile on his lips. "Just think, Ben, when some of your rural parishioners decide to hold a

Christmas event, I bet the only thing they expect you to do is turn up, smile, and bless everything."

I can't help a slight laugh. He's right. Rural priests' time is strictly reserved for actual sacraments. No administrative duties beyond managing their own schedules. It definitely has that in common with hospital or prison ministry. More time going directly into soul-care.

"Oh, this is cool, you have a priest hole." Tommy's gone back to flipping through the manual. "A refuge certified to give three to five hours protection from raptors, depending on various factors. Let's see, how do we… No, you do it." He shoves the book at me. "You need to know how."

After some fiddling around, I manage to raise a long panel from the center of the aisle, revealing a small, man-sized compartment deep in the chassis. Tommy's keen to climb in and try it for size and have me put the lid on but, when I lift it again, he climbs out with his already pale skin a shade or two paler.

"Sheesh, that's like being in a—" He breaks off, pasting an unfelt grin on his face. "Well, that's a heck of a good thing to have. You don't need armor if you've got that."

It's only after he's helped me carry a few boxes down to the van and dashed off to answer a ping from the hospital that I lift the refuge lid again and squeeze

into it myself. I barely fit. I guess it's made for someone more Jerry's size.

I practice getting the lid down a few times, then lie there for a while, imagining I'm unSPARKed, raptors scratching at the van doors. It's not a relaxing exercise. There's a little light in here and I turn it on and off a few times, before deciding that it's better with it off.

It's bad enough being able to feel that you're lying in a coffin without being able to see it too.

+

The line at the city gate is shorter than I was afraid it might be. The main holiday rush, people traveling to see relatives, hasn't fully begun yet. Things wriggle in my belly as I look at the great city-fence ahead, like worms in a decaying corpse, which I might be soon enough…

Sheesh, Ben, morbid, much? Get a grip. Father Gestadt is still alive, isn't he?

Kinda.

It's just after midday, Saturday. Five days until Christmas. After a frenetic week of organizing and discarding and moving, too many dreams and not enough sleep, the van is packed, my remaining stuff has been dumped at Sanctuary House, still in boxes except for a few old rally trophies that I shoved on the side table to try to make it feel homey, and it's time to go.

The carol service-baptism tonight is at a farm only about a three-hour drive from Exception City, according to the navigation system, but night falls early at this time of year and it will probably take me longer than that since the last hour is on unmonitored minor roads. Poorly maintained and unfamiliar, so I'll have to go steady. No rally notes, no navigator to help me, and if I crash out there it won't be eager helpers swarming the vehicle.

Too soon, I'm showing my pass to the gate inspection official, forcing myself to lounge casually at the wheel like I'm okay with this—and then I'm being waved through.

And I'm unSPARKed. For the first time since the Green Acres breach.

Lord, help me!

As I accelerate onto the highway, I glance up at the little Guardian Angel shield clipped to my visor—I must check if Jerry meant to leave that for me—and my own Marian shield beside it, and I murmur an appeal to both. *Lord, watch over me.* Then my gaze shifts to that fateful claw necklace of mine hanging from the rear-view screen, before drifting to the little statuette on the dashboard, a man in a brown tunic and jeans holding a double-armful of little 'saurs cradled to his chest. Babies or miniature adults, I'm not sure which they're meant to represent.

"Saint Desmond, pray for me," I whisper out loud.

I guess I really am a rural priest, now.

+

Driving on the main monitored highway is as dull as I remember from the rare occasions I actually did it pre-Green Acres. Although I watch the highway signs closely for updates, everything remains quiet. I glimpse a herd of triceratops feeding on a distant hillside, but that's as wildlifey as it gets.

Since I re-read the Highway Safety Info booklet yesterday, my brain decides to occupy the time composing a more realistic version.

-If you break down, call Highway Patrol as soon as you get a satellite lock to request assistance…

If you break down, say an Act of Perfect Contrition immediately to ensure you're ready to meet your Maker.

I remember how funny some of the guys in the 'Vi-park found the idea of waiting for Highway Patrol.

"Do you know how often satellites actually pass over some rural areas?" they would laugh. "Never!"

- Preparation is everything. Before traveling unSPARKed, ensure you have securely fixed window grilles and wheel shields. It is best to travel unSPARKed in a suitably protected vehicle in case of a break-down near raptors…

Preparation is everything. Before traveling unSPARKed, ensure you have made a good confession. It is best to travel unSPARKed in a state of grace in case of consumption by raptors.

Bishop Dennis gave me absolution yesterday, so I've dealt with that one.

-Always travel on fully-monitored roads. Avoid unmonitored minor roads…

Always keep to the straight and narrow path. Avoid the broad and easy route.

Hang on, that one's kind of backwards…

Never mind. I'm starting to bore myself. I almost put the radio on, then remember that unnecessary noise is a bad idea. *Nothing to see here, carni'saurs.*

After two hours on the highway I finally turn off, passing under massive signs warning that I'm now leaving the monitored route and if I insist on going this way I should be careful not to have an emergency because they can't promise when—or even if—I'll get help.

Abandon hope, all ye who enter here…

Oh shut up, Ben. It's your first trip. Nothing is likely to happen!

This is a well-travelled route, anyway, not like the infamous track through the now not-so-far-distant mountains that hunter rally drivers reportedly drive for practice—or just for fun. Precipices everywhere and very little chance of ever acquiring satellite lock to call for help.

This 'major' minor road is considerably less well-maintained than the highway, even so, with potholes, loose bits, wet stretches, and a few areas that could barely be called paved. The mild weather means there's little risk of ice—not before full night has fallen, at any rate. The technical challenge of driving absorbs all my concentration and soon—if I'm honest—I'm enjoying myself. The van wouldn't win any races for speed, but it's a workhorse, chugging steadily up the inclines and gripping well on the descents. Soon I'm talking to it the way I would my rally car or my Fury. I'm bonding with the chunky thing faster than I thought I would.

"Yeah, we can do this," I murmur. "Slow and steady wins the race. Of life, anyway… I wouldn't win any rallies in you, would I? But you're a trier."

It's kind of exciting, driving alone through the wilderness like this. I glimpse more wildlife now. Some bushy-feathered things like ostriches with tails... A herd of much larger herbi'saurs but I can't remember if the beaky mouths mean they're edmontosaurs or iguanodons…

What's *that?* Heart pounding, I let the van roll to a halt. A large, distant, upright silhouette moves across a slope in the light of the dropping sun. Is that an allosaur? A young T. rex? Am I supposed to stop? Yeah.

But the predator moves on its way without showing any interest in the far-away van, so I let out a long breath along with the clutch and go on my way.

+

This is hardly a rally-track, the road's too good for that, but still, I haven't had this much fun driving for a long time, on those perfect city roads. A pang of disappointment actually strikes me when another vehicle appears on the road ahead. A slower vehicle. I ease back to make sure I'm not following too close.

From the inexpert driving and the look of the fragile city-vehicle with its light-weight window grilles, it's a city-family on their way to visit rural relatives for Christmas. Or maybe on their way to a resort for the holiday season.

Light-weight window grilles, huh? I didn't even have any grilles on my Fury—no plans to drive it unSPARKed, oddly enough—but I already compare the ones ahead to the ones on the van and see the difference. The van sports heavy duty grilles, like a farm truck, I guess. Visibly more substantial.

But still only designed to provide good protection to a moving vehicle…

I push that thought from my head and concentrate on not closing the gap and crowding the nervous driver ahead. No space to pass them.

From the increasingly erratic nature of their driving, they're going faster than their ability really allows. I'm staying well back, so they must be racing the dusk. The sun is very low in the sky, now. I've got less than an hour to go, so I'm okay, but maybe they need to go further. This road in the dark might be a little too much excitement even for me.

Even for me? Maybe Tommy's right. Maybe I do like a little adrenalin in my life.

+

The light keeps dropping. The road gets worse. But the car ahead goes faster and faster. I frown as I watch them skid around another corner. *Come on, you've got headlights, it's not worth crashing.*

But who says they'll drive any better once the stress of the darkness settles around them? Headlights show only the road ahead. You could drive straight past a rex at night and not know it until it started peeling your car open like a sardine can.

No, this is crazy. They're bombing up a steep incline with reckless speed. Maybe I should get on the interCar radio and ask how far they're going? I might be able to follow them to their destination. Safety in numbers. Though that'll leave me driving back to my own destination in the dark, like as not. But I'm okay for time, so I'd better try. Odds are I'll just offend them. But it's not like they're going to get out and come throw a punch, like in the city. Although, most guys re-think throwing a punch, when they clap eyes on me properly. Sometimes being big and broad is an advantage.

I pause before I can press the button. It looks like a tight corner up there. I'd better let them get around that first before I risk distracting them.

The rear of the city-car slides wildly as they reach the crest and disappears too suddenly from view. Frowning, heart leaping to my mouth, I gun the engine, reaching the summit a little quicker than I would otherwise have done. But the sound of metal hitting rock greets me as I come up over the top.

Too late. Easing off the gas, I inch down the slippery road toward where the little car rests at the bottom of the incline, its hood crumpled up against a great slab of rock. Deep tire marks score down the muddy road surface where their brakes failed to stop their excessive momentum. Heck.

Lord, let them be okay…

But my belly's tense. They hit hard. I want to believe they might be okay, but…they may not be. I ease the van alongside the crashed vehicle, peering through those light grilles as I try to get a look inside. Two figures slump in the front seats. And is that…my gut tenses even more. I think there's a baby's car seat in the back.

Outage.

I glance at the WhatHap box in the center of the dash console, but there's no satellite signal. Scanning the wilderness around me, I check for movement, danger, any signs of life. Nothing. But there could be twenty raptors out there and I wouldn't have the experience to spot them. Highway rules state that I stay in my vehicle, wait for a satellite lock and then call this in. But who knows how long that will take?

I peer at the car seat again. A baby. Heck. If I get this wrong…will I ever forgive myself? Will the parents? They'll probably *sue* me. Nah, if this goes wrong I won't be alive to be sued. And…I'm not in the city anymore. There's no guarantee if or when anyone will come to help us. *Weigh the odds*, that's what the hunters say, isn't it? You can't be sure it will go right, so you just take the best odds. And the first thing Isaiah Wilson did once he had me and little Mei Ling in his Hab'Vi was to…

Okay. I look all around again, swallow, then climb into the back. *Get everything ready first, Ben…*

Fumbling in my haste, I find the first aid kit and my sick call kit and put them both beside the sliding door, then I get the refuge lid up. Peering out the living area window, I check the landscape again, one last time, then roll back the sliding door. The sound of crying strikes my ears, making panic spike. If I can hear it, so can… *Quickly!*

A few steps take me to the crashed car. *Oh God, let this be right!* I open the rear door and lean inside.

"I have a refuge," I say, loudly and clearly. "I'm putting your baby into it."

No response from the front, but I don't wait, I just grab the car seat fixings and unfasten them, lifting the whole thing out, baby and all. If the poor mite's hurt, this is less likely to harm it.

"It's okay," I croon, turning and moving the few steps back to the van, laden with my precious cargo. "It's okay, little one."

I lean into the van and slide the car seat down into the refuge. Get the lid down, muffling the screaming at last. *Click, click, click*, go the three catches. Right, that's the baby in the safest possible place. I straighten, grab the two kits, and slide the van door closed, clicking the key once to safety-lock it so raptors can't open the doors just by playing with the handles. Not twice to secure-lock it, of course. Rescuers need to be able to get in.

A few steps and I'm scrambling into the back of the car and pulling the door closed. Sweat drips into my eyes, and I'm starting to shake. But I've done it. I've got the baby into the refuge. It didn't go horribly, horribly wrong… *Thank you, Lord, thank you.*

Now for the parents.

I scramble forward and lean between the front seats. One glance at the young woman in the passenger seat and my chest clenches. Her head lolls, turned at an improbable angle, and her eyes are blank and fixed. Prayer is the only way I can help her now.

I switch my attention to the young man behind the wheel. His head lolls too, but at a less twisted angle, and I see his chest rise and fall slightly in the dim light. He's breathing. But the front of the car and the wheel are pushed right into him, blocking any view of his lower half, and a strong metallic scent fills the air. Blood? I don't like his odds.

I open the first aid kit and pull out the contents booklet. I haven't even had time to look through this kit yet.

x6 'No-shock' patch

Yeah, I'm familiar with those. I rip one open, peel off the backing and stick it to his neck. Hard to imagine it helping much. He needs morphine.

Hang on…

x3 morphine injections for more serious injuries

Huh, rural first aid kits are a step above city ones. Clumsily, I inject him with a syringeful. Hopefully that will help more.

Hang on… A light has just started flashing on the center of the dash, coming from the rugged, self-powered WhatHap box which has survived the impact unscathed. Satellite lock! I lung forward and press the emergency button.

Nothing.

Nothing.

Nothing…

"Hello, this is Highway Patrol, what is your emergency?"

"There's been a car wreck. The woman's dead, the man is badly injured. I've put the baby into the refuge of my van."

"Refuge?"

"It's an SOS van; I'm a priest. The refuge is under the floor of the living area."

"And where are you now?" I hear keys tapping as she notes it all down.

"In the car with the injured man."

She tuts slightly but doesn't waste signal time telling me off for all this wandering around. "We'll dispatch a patrol car to your location immediately. Stay still and quiet. If it's dark before they arrive, avoid showing lights or doing anything that might attract attention." A hesitation, then she adds, probably off-script, "Some might advise moving back to the SOS van if that has stronger grilles."

"I can't move the man, he's pinned."

"Understood. Up to you whether you stay with him, then, especially if he's bleeding—" Her voice cuts off. The signal is gone.

I let out a long breath. How long will it take them to reach us?

"Ummph…" The man is struggling to raise his head, moaning slightly. "Wha…? What's…?"

"Try not to move too much," I say quickly. "You've sustained injuries in a car accident. What's your name?"

"Huh?"

"I'm Father Ben. What's your name?"

"Craig…"

"Hello, Craig." I keep my voice calm and friendly. "I'm sorry to meet you under such circumstances. What's your little boy's name?" I'm guessing at the gender but the baby clothes were blue.

"Craig, Jr.! *Where*…?" He's looking around frantically, now, squinting as though he can't see well.

"He's safe, Craig. He's in the refuge in my van. I'm a priest. I have a very strong refuge and he's tucked away in there. Highway Patrol know he's in there. He'll be fine until they arrive. Don't worry about little Craig, Jr. He's very safe."

He relaxes for a fraction of a second, then tenses again, trying to see past me. "Helen? How's Helen?"

Something taps my face as I try to keep my body between him and the dead woman. Huh, a little rosary hangs from the rear-view mirror. That makes up my mind on how to answer. Because I've got to answer…

"I'm very sorry, Craig. She's with God."

"What? No… *No*…" His voice cracks.

"I'm sorry. I think she broke her neck in the accident. She didn't suffer." Too many Catholics nowadays find the idea of a sudden, unprovided—but painless—death attractive, which is a horror and tragedy, in my opinion—but I'll use what comfort I can to lessen the shock.

"No… I…I don't know what happened… The car slid… No, she can't be…"

"The slope was treacherous. You couldn't have anticipated it." He was going too fast, but the slope *was* the worst on the road so far. Nothing I say is going to stop him feeling guilty so there's no need to turn the knife.

"Are you Catholic?" I ask gently, hoping to distract him and direct his thoughts to what I suspect is his very most pressing concern—the state of his soul.

"Uh…Helen is…was…" His voice shakes and almost breaks. "I…uh…I used to be. I don't go to church anymore."

"Had Helen been to confession recently?" I'm not that hopeful about the reply. Many people who take their faith fairly seriously still don't darken the door of the confessional more than once or twice a year.

"Last Saturday…I think."

Huh. Thanks, Lord.

"That must be very consoling for you." Never mind that he doesn't go to church anymore…

"Uh…" Confusion covers his face then clears a little. "I guess…it's good."

"May I ask, Craig, why you don't go to church anymore?"

He eyes me, his pupils still struggling to focus. "You really want to talk about this now, Father?"

"Yes, Craig, I do."

He's silent for a while, trying to focus down at himself, at me again. When he speaks again his voice quavers. "Father? I'm hurt bad, aren't I?"

"I'm not a doctor, but I suspect so. I gave you a dose of morphine to reduce the pain."

He makes a ragged sobbing noise in his throat, then sits for a while, his breath whistling in and out, muttering brokenly to himself. I make out "Helen" and "Craig, Jr." quite a few times, like he doesn't even know if he wants to stay or go.

"Millie, my sister…" Eventually he speaks a bit louder. "She's…she's wanted a baby for so long. Ever so long. She and Greg. They'll…they'll look after Craig, Jr. They'll…they'll look after him…"

I think he's talking more to himself, but I smile anyway. "That's great, Craig. Knowing he's going to be loved and cared for, whatever happens."

"He's safe? You're sure he's—"

"Highway Patrol are already on their way, and the refuge is good for five hours. He's perfectly safe." And from the volume of his crying, he's probably not hurt, either.

"So," I say gently, hoping to direct things back to Craig Senior, "why did you stop going to Mass?"

He tries to focus on me again. "It was just so…inconvenient. My land-surfing, y'know? The guys liked to go to the city surf park on…on Sunday mornings. Helen…uh, she helped with the Children's Church in the morning. So, uh…I had to go by myself in the evening. And, uh…the guys…they thought that was hilarious. So I…uh…" He pauses, seeming confused, then grasps his thread again and rushes on. "Eventually I just stopped going. Helen was…was so upset with me but that just…it just made me more stubborn. Why was I like that? It hurt her so…so much. Helen, Helen, I'm so sorry…"

He starts sobbing in earnest. Sobbing and moaning. The movement is hurting him. I grip his shoulder gently, trying to soothe him.

"Shss, Craig, it's alright. It's alright. Would you like me to hear your confession and make things right with God so you can be with Helen?"

His sobs trail off as though they're too much to sustain, and he whispers in a very small voice, "Yes, please."

I make sure he tells me only the few most serious sins to avoid him exhausting himself further, then absolve him. I'm not a doctor, I can't be absolutely sure he's dying, and I don't want to harm his chances if things aren't as serious as they look.

I follow up with Anointing of the Sick, and when we're done, a glance at the WhatHap shows it's only been fifteen minutes since I placed the call. Depending on where the nearest dispatch station is, it's hard to believe they could be here in less than an hour. Forty-five minutes, bare minimum. So we've at least half an hour to kill, probably more. And it's still light enough to see.

"Don't carry Consecrated Hosts," Bishop Dennis told me when I saw him. "Not unless you're certain the Sacrament will be needed very urgently when you arrive somewhere. You've enough to think about in the event of a breakdown without worrying if raptors are going to desecrate Our Lord."

"I'd like to say Mass for you," I tell Craig. He won't be receiving viaticum any other way. "Is that okay?"

He blinks in confusion. "Right here?"

"Of course. I have everything I need."

"Uh...sure..."

I open my sick call kit and set things up on the misshapen dash. Once I begin, I refuse to rush in an unseemly manner, though my knees ache from squatting on the parking brake like this, and my hips and lower back protest being twisted into the space between the seats with an increasingly fiery ache.

Every word of this Mass seems to have such...weight...as it comes from my lips. *Reality of all realities...*

I keep up a respectfully respectable pace as Craig fades in and out of consciousness. But he's awake as I place a small fragment of the Host on his tongue at the end, and he watches me clearing everything away with his slightly unfocused gaze.

"That was the best Mass I've ever…" he mutters at last, his words slurring slightly.

"Except your nuptial Mass, I'm sure." I give him a grin and a gentle wink and get a slight smile back.

"Maybe even…'cluding that," he mumbles—and falls silent again.

A few minutes later, I realize I can't hear his strained breathing anymore, but it's so dark in the car now I'm unable to see if his chest is moving. I have to search for his pulse.

I can't find it.

+

I murmur a quick prayer for Craig's repose, and Helen's too, eyeing the gathering twilight outside the car. Should I transfer back to the van? There's no longer any reason to stay in the less secure vehicle. Could I fit in the refuge with Craig Jr., if I took him out of his car seat?

Visibility is getting very limited, though. Getting out again is risky. On the other hand, if there was something out there it would probably have its face against the window by now, trying to get to the blood. It's probably worth the risk.

I wriggle my bulk back into the rear of the car, where I can easily reach a door, and take one more look, but it really is too gloomy to see very far. I take a deep breath and open the door. Two legs out, straighten…

Something feathery lunges out of the gloom with an eager screech.

I swing on pure instinct, roaring wildly, my fist smacking painfully into a bony jaw. Screech turning into more of a squeal, the creature darts away, then swings around to look at me as I topple backwards into the car, grabbing at the door.

Quick, quick, quick…!

The raptor just stares warily as my fingers close around the door handle. *Pull. Click.*

Heck, that was close. I stare out at the bizarrely pathetic raptor. It let me get away? Seriously? Just because I bopped it on the nose? What kind is it? I learned something about raptors at Green Acres, from Isaiah and Zechariah, and I read a little afterwards so I knew more about my pair of claws. It's brown, so a Dakotaraptor, right? Like my claws… But it's too small, its head only coming up to my chest. Deinonychus? I thought their heads were dome-shaped. I take in the hint of fluffiness about its profile, and it clicks. Yeah, Dakotaraptor. But a juvenile. Huh. No wonder it didn't know what to make of me.

What do I do? Stay put? If the rest of the pack come they can have these puny grilles off long before Highway Patrol arrive. No, there's just one juvenile out there, already wary of me. The refuge is my only chance, I have to reach it. I should have jumped into the van instead of back in here.

I grope around in the bottom of the car, under the seats, hoping for a tire iron, but all I come up with is a long handled ice-scraper. That'll have to do. Any weapon is better than nothing — might keep the skittish thing a bit further away from me.

Ice-scraper tightly clenched in my hand, I reach for the door handle just as the juvenile screeches happily and bounds forward with those terrifyingly bouncy, ground-eating strides I remember all too well. And there…coming to meet it…two adults. As tall as me and many times longer from nose to tail-tip.

Fresh sweat breaks out all over me and I take my hand away from the door handle. Too slow. I've been too slow. Or maybe just-enough slow. If I'd jumped out a moment earlier…

Yeah, supper would have been served.

+

Coated in sweat and with the temperature plummeting as night draws in, I'm shaking hard as cold and fear grip me. But my brain insists on supplying dialogue as the juvenile meets its visibly disgruntled parents.

Juvenile: Mom, Dad, look—

Mom: How many times have I told you not to wander off?

Juvenile: But Mom—

Dad: It's not safe. What if you met a rex?

Juvenile: But Mom, Dad, look, look what I found! It's a whole can of food. Look!

The juvenile hops back to the car, cocking its head, snatching lightly at the grilles with its teeth. *Look, Mom, Dad, see! There's food inside. How do we open it?*

The adults join the youngster. It's too dark to see their eye color, but I get a good look at their leathery faces as they peer in at me. I sit very still. Movement bad, right? Triggers hunting instinct…

The accusatory noises from the adults die away as they focus on the car. Their brightly colored ruffs flare eagerly. Maybe Junior's done good after all.

Nothing to it, Junior. Watch and learn. The smaller adult, which I'm assuming is the dad, grips a grille and yanks hard. The car rocks violently. The grille makes a slight screechy noise, but holds.

Is it better to move and risk exciting them, or just let them get on with it unopposed? A bleak voice whispers that there's so much blood in this car nothing short of a rifle is going to drive them off.

As the female reaches for the rear grille, I put out my hand and press the window button, hoping to drop the glass so I can jab at her with my puny ice-scraper— but the window doesn't respond. The car systems are trashed.

That settles that, then. I just sit here and wait.

Yank. She's stronger than the male and the car rocks even harder, the grille making a faint groaning sound. Yeah. It's not going to take them that long to get them off or break through them. All three raptors look thin and scrawny. If I recollect from my reading, a tiny family like this must be an old matriarch and her mate, trying to raise one last brood on the peripheries of larger packs' territories.

I grope through the footwells again, frantically hunting for something more dangerous than the ice-scraper, but there's nothing. All I find is a car blanket, thrown to the floor by the impact. Wrapping it around me, I huddle in the middle of the back seat, clutching my pitiful weapon.

Only now that it's about to happen do I realize that the thing I've been belly-aching and stressing about ever since the bishop's meeting wasn't something I really, truly, deep-down thought would actually happen. Not to me.

God's allowed to call your number, y'know. Tommy's voice echoes in my head.

Is that why I've been so grumpy about all this? It wasn't just swapping my car and my comfy city-life for the discomforts of life on the road. It was having to face up to the truth of what Tommy said. I gave my life to God in a very special way when I said yes to the priesthood—but even if I was a layperson still, He's got the right to take me any time, like a Farmer plucking a grain of wheat from a field because He decide it's ripe—or just feels like it.

Despite all the homilies I've given, all the wise words I've spoken to those with serious diagnoses, all the comfort I've offered grieving families, have I truly accepted it, for me, for myself? That I don't get a say in this?

Guess not.

Couldn't you have just given me a meaningful scripture verse or something, Lord? This seems kinda drastic.

Maybe I'm so thick and pig-headed only the two-by-four approach would work.

Sorry, Lord. I huddle into my blanket as the three raptors rock and shake the car. *My number's yours to call. I get it.*

This is going to be one of the shortest careers as a rural priest since the 'Rewilding,' as the hunters call it. Talk about bad luck.

Probably not luck, though, is it? And—I glance at the still, slumped silhouettes in the front—not *bad* luck, either. Craig Jr. is saved and Craig Sr. is saved, if in different ways, because I was right here, right now. Why do I even think this is about *me*?

I hope I've done what you wanted, Lord. Getting killed on day one feels like bad resource management, but what price a soul and a life, I guess?

Squeak-creak…

My gaze jerks to the driver's window grille, which the raptors are paying particular attention to—and my heart rate kicks up. The bars are buckling in the middle. It won't be long, now. Is there any chance at all I can stay quiet in the back and they'll eat Craig and Helen and go on their way?

Dream on, Ben.

Absolution last night or not, I say an Act of Contrition, as perfect as I can make it. My teeth are chattering and I can't even tell if it's more the cold or the fear.

Keep little Craig Jr. safe, Lord. Get him to his aunt and uncle…

Creak… The middle bar tears right away, leaving a six-inch gap. Not large enough for them to get their head through, but large enough to give them a lot more leverage on the other bars.

Outage, how much is this going to hurt?

Less than a crucifixion.

That would go for pretty much every death, but… yeah. I fish out my rosary and try to pray, since it's probably the only way to stop my whining.

Squeak. Another bar gives way. The female thrusts her muzzle into the gap, snapping eagerly, but she can't quite reach poor Craig.

Hail Mary, full of grace…

Snap. A mighty yank and the next bar breaks away at one end. It's still blocking them, but it won't take them long to bend it…

Now and at the hour of our…

The raptors pause, their heads rising as though they're listening. The parents run a few paces, look back, call to their chick. *Come!* The juvenile bites at the grille, making fretful sounds. *Want dinner now!* The female raptor springs back and nips her naughty offspring, herding him ahead of her. And they're gone into the darkness.

My heart pounding like a jackhammer, I edge closer to the window and peer after them. What are they running from? A rex? A full pack of Dakotaraptors?

Should I try to get into the van? The car's providing no protection at all, now. I may jump straight into the teeth of something else, but I'm dead if I stay.

With a sudden burst of determination, I throw the rear door open; leap out, brandishing my ice-scraper like a rapier, my two kits clutched in my other hand like a shield. The blanket falls from my shoulders— *brrr*—but I turn toward the van door…

Light blazes across my face and a second later the roar of an engine reaches my ears as a vehicle crests the summit above. I stand, unable to move, staring as though seeing a vision.

Not a rex, not a pack…

With effort, I snap out of it, sliding the van door open and jumping inside. *Click.* I'm in. Instead of going to the refuge, I climb through into the front seat and look out as the dazzling vehicle, the wonderful vehicle, makes a careful descent and draws alongside. Luminous hi-vis stripes cover the sides. Highway Patrol. I'd almost forgotten about them; I was so sure they'd be too late.

Oh my. Thank you, Lord.

The patrol vehicle reverses up to the rock face, then drives a complete half-circle around my van and the crashed car. Little poles plop from the back, weighted at the bottom so they stand upright, bobbing from side-to-side. Presumably wires join them together, though I can't see them in the darkness. When the semi-circle is complete the vehicle pulls back over to the van and a moment later little red flashing lights activate on top of the poles. The temporary fence is live.

It's darn low, thinking of the size of those Dakotaraptors. But few animals are quick to mess with electricity.

In the flickering red light, I make out the silhouette of a figure popping up into the domed cage that sticks from the roof of the vehicle, a figure holding a long thin rifle. We've got a fence—and cover.

Only now do the doors of the patrol truck open and several hi-vis clad figures pour out. One of them comes straight to my door, so I lower my window.

"You just fancied a stroll or something?" an ironic voice greets me. They must've seen me standing there like a rabbit in the headlights.

"The raptors ran off when they heard you coming so I thought I'd better get back in the van. Look what they did to the window." I point at the car.

"Yikes. How's the casualty?"

"Dead, I'm afraid. He was half crushed."

"And the baby?"

"Still in the refuge. I think he was probably uninjured but you'd better take a look right away."

I return to the rear of the vehicle and open the side door, then lift the refuge lid. A fresh wave of crying greets the noise and the chill night air—at least, I hope he hasn't been screaming in here this whole time, though it's possible—and when I lift the car seat out and hand it to the patrolman he double-times it back to their vehicle and climbs inside.

"His name's Craig, Jr.," I call to a second patrol…woman as she follows close behind.

As the other patrollers swarm over the car, I sit there numbly on the van floor for a while and shiver, ambushed by a desperate, desperate desire to go *home*. Right. This. Minute. Eventually the realization sinks in that I *am* home—I'll never be at that little suite in Sanctuary House enough for that to become home—so what am I waiting for?

I scrape myself off the floor, close the door, put the kettle on, then sit on the bed with a quilt wrapped around me and the heater turned up, sipping my hot coffee and eating a chocolate bar from the house-warming candy Tommy stuffed my drawers with. After a while I get out my Office book and say Evening Prayer, since I'm not sure when I'll have another chance.

Eventually a patroller rolls the sliding door open again and looks in. "Baby's fine as far as we can tell. I'm afraid I can confirm that the people in the car are deceased. We've transferred them to our storage facility. Are you alright? Is your van?"

"Fine. I wasn't involved in the accident and the raptors never got to me." Not quite.

"Good. We'll take the car in tow and remove it immediately; get the baby to the hospital ASAP for a proper check-up."

"There's an aunt and uncle to take charge of the little man. Millie and Greg."

The patrolman whips out a hand-pad to note this down. "Thank you; that might speed things up. If you're okay, we'll leave you to it. We'll be taking the fence down before we go; just move on when you're ready."

Just move on when I'm ready? Do they whip the fence down and leave normal cars sitting around in the dark in the middle of nowhere? I guess it's because I'm a priest in an SOS van. They assume this is all in a day's work for me. The fact that I'm sitting here with my mug and my prayer book probably just confirms that, as far as they're concerned.

Huh… "I'm sorry; I should have offered you all a hot drink."

The patrolman waves this away. "No time. We need to wrap this up and get ready for our next dispatch. It's the holiday silly season, Father; you know what it's like. Every year you'd think there was a competition how many people can slab themselves just before Christmas. But thanks for the offer."

Yep, he definitely thinks I'm an old hand at all this. Of course, even in my fairly brief priestly career I've rushed to the bedside—more often morgue-side—of a fair few parishioners who've been in accidents or muggings. And yet, rural life is seen as so much more dangerous…

It's definitely nice to have been in time for once. Too often, comforting the relatives is the most one can do after something like this. And however important and desperately needed that is, for a priest it's a secondary priority.

Minutes later, what's left of the car is hitched to the back of the truck, the fence is gone, and they're roaring away. And I'm left alone in the dark with my van and my cup of Joe.

+

I finish my coffee quickly, climb back into the front, switch on the headlights, start the engine, and get under way before the raptors can come back.

Tap, tap, tap, my claw necklace swings against the windshield as we move along. I force my attention onto the road, refusing to think about what might be watching me from the darkness. The only thing within my control is to make sure I don't end like Craig and Helen, especially since it's getting to ice o'clock now.

Thanks to the coffee and my van heater, I've just about stopped shivering. As the driving absorbs my concentration, my insides gradually stop quivering too.

I'm alive. Guess it was just a teaching moment after all.

Or all in a day's work.

Huh. It dawns on me that I'm *all right*. I mean, not just alive and well, but…

I didn't enjoy that. I don't relish the thought of it happening again. But I am all right. I'm heading on my way, I've a baby to baptize, carols to sing, new parishioners to meet. And I'm okay.

Maybe everyone is right. Maybe I *can* cope with this job, after all.

+

Despite my alrightness, when I come over the top of an incline and see, far out ahead on a valley floor, a little cluster of buildings blazing with light, and realize it's the farm I'm aiming for, a choking wave of relief sweeps over me. I force myself to go on driving slow and careful.

Baptism, next. No, a *conditional* baptism. I run through the less familiar words in my head, practicing. Fortunately, I'm now in possession of a booklet entitled 'Diocese of Exception State, Combined Rites for Rural Use' which tells me how this baptism-carol service is supposed to go—and a whole lot of increasingly bizarre sacramental combinations, besides. Baptisms during a Requiem Mass, anyone? Do hunters figure that if they've got to let the priest into their camp to bury Grandpa, they might as well get all the kids done at the same time?

"Eighty percent of Catholic farmers have Mary or Desmond for their middle names," I remember Gerry telling me. "Catholic hunters, though, a whopping ninety-five percent have Mary Desmond for the guys and Mary Desmelda for the girls. And don't bother trying to tell them that isn't the feminine form of Desmond; as far as they're concerned it is. Uh…don't expect variety in middle names, I suppose that's what I'm saying. Um…why am I telling you this? Oh. A baptism. That's the thing not to miss. On Saturday…"

Will this little farmgirl be a Something Mary Something? Probably.

Soon, I'm passing under a line of fence toplights winking high above me and following a long drive through flat pastures. Finally I draw to a halt outside the gate of the inner fence.

Taking a deep breath—*come on, body, now is not the time to break down and sob*—I press the InterCar button to ping the farmhouse.

"Hello the gate?" A woman's voice answers almost at once.

"Hello, this is Father Benedict."

"Ah, good, we were getting worried. Turned on all the lights in case you were lost. Come on in, Father."

The gate slides open. I drive forward, then pause and wait while the first gate closes and a second opens. Forward again. Aaaand…I'm SPARKed again. I have to pull to a halt for a moment and lean on the steering wheel, drawing in a few long, deep breaths.

Made it. *I made it.*

+

Friendly faces.

Coats and rifles line the hall.

Hot cider.

Pecan pie.

Warmth.

Safety.

Too many names…

"We're just here for the food," says a stocky young man who—ever-so-cheerfully—makes a point of calling me 'Ben' all the time, his arm wrapped around his wife's shoulders. "And the christening, of course.

Seeing that we're the hope-never-to-be guardians, and all. But we're leaving the God-stuff to them." He jabs a thumb at another neighbor-couple.

"We're the Godparents, Father!" beams the woman, her teeth white against her rich dark skin.

Apparently, who would be guardian is a publically recognized role, out here. Though even in my slightly dazed state, I wonder why it's to be the atheist neighbors instead of the Catholic Godparents—then realize it's probably to do with money. Mr. Making-a-point-of-calling-me-Ben and his well-dressed wife look like they could easily afford to feed an extra mouth—the Godparents rather less so. Or maybe it's customary to share the roles among the closest friends, so no one feels passed over.

"Time to start," our hosts are calling, as they attempt to shepherd everyone into a family room from which chairs overflow into the hall. "Father Benedict, come, have you had enough pie?"

I assure them I've had all I can eat, and I'm ushered to the front of the family room, where a large mixing bowl has been transformed into a font by the addition of something resembling a white silk Christmas tree skirt. Soon everyone is settled and we launch into the opening hymn.

Craig and Helen and Craig Jr. I run through their names in my head so I can include them in the intercessory prayers. But first…

The hymn draws to a close and a baby girl is placed into my arms. I expect the usual crisp brand-new gown in the latest style but, no. This country child squirms in a long white heirloom baptismal gown decorated with a tasteful trim of white rabbit fur, probably worn by every generation of this family, since before the Rewilding.

My heart swells as I carefully hold the little one over the make-shift font and scoop water over her head. This is a much happier way to end my first day.

"Darryl Mary Franklyn," I recite clearly, "if you are not already baptized then I baptize you in the name of the Father, and of the Son, and of the Holy Spirit."

It's a new beginning for this little one, a new life — at least officially. And for me too.

Lord, let me learn to love this job, if it is Your will.

Because I'm actually beginning to believe that might be possible, after all.

Just one problem remains, one so insurmountable that I've been refusing to think about it at all.

How do I tell my mom?

To read about Father Ben's adventure at Green Acres breach, don't miss the prequel novel BREACH!
And to see how Father Ben's life as a country priest is going, make sure you pick up the novel A VERY JURASSIC CHRISTMAS.

A NOTE FROM THE AUTHOR

I wrote 'A Very Jurassic Lent' for the Catholic Teen Books Lenten anthology, ASHES: VISIBLE & INVISIBLE, which was released early in 2023. 'A Very Jurassic Lent' takes place during the time period covered by A RIGHT REX RODEO. Look out for a few references to the events in the short story early on in that book.

A VERY JURASSIC LENT

TIME: DURING BOOK 6 OF THE MAIN unSPARKed SERIES (A RIGHT REX RODEO).

HARRY

"So I just toss it up into the air?" I eye the contents of the frying pan.

"What? No!" Josh takes the pan from the stovetop and gives it an exploratory shake, making the pancake slide from side to side with a papery sound. "You have to do it just the right way so you can *catch* the pancake again. Watch, I'll do this one."

He steps into the open part of the Habitat Vehicle's living area—such as it is with the table out—then gives the pan a sharp flick. The pancake soars up into the air, turns over—and drops neatly back into the pan, uncooked side now downwards.

Darryl smiles and claps, then raises a hand to

stroke Kiko, who had recoiled slightly at Josh's sudden movement, hunching into his four long wing-limbs. The little quadravian—or microraptor as their scientific name is—quickly relaxes, settling more comfortably on her shoulder.

Nope, my big sis doesn't look at all bothered that we're about to try doing what Josh just did. I am definitely going to drop mine.

"Remind me again why we don't just turn them over with a spatula?" I say.

"Tossing pancakes on Shrove Tuesday is traditional," says Josh. "And it's more fun."

"Isn't any Fat Tuesday tradition I've ever heard of." And spending all evening clearing up pancake from the floor or ceiling isn't what I'd call fun, either. We do enough cleaning as it is, cat-like, trying to avoid the notice of any predator large enough to breach the Habitat Vehicle.

"It's a hunter tradition. This guy came over from Britain soon after the Rewilding and married into a big hunter family and brought it with him. Soon everyone were doing it. And...there we are." He slides the finished pancake onto a plate and holds out the empty pan, glancing from me to Darryl. "I tossed it, I getta eat it. Who wants the next one?"

I want the next one, I just don't want to toss it, so I let Darryl take the frying pan. Josh only has one—no space for clutter in a HabVi.

Josh ladles out some of the edmontosaur mince that's keeping warm in the OmniProcessor and rolls the pancake up neatly.

Darryl pauses, pushing her long brown braid behind her back, and gives me a meaningful look. Oh, right, it's my turn to say grace. Once I've finished, Josh digs in.

Of course, Darryl tosses her pancake so neatly you'd think she was hunter-born not farmer-born. And then it's my turn.

I catch it! With an undignified lunge, but I catch it. They clap and don't laugh—much.

"So, what do Hunters eat on Ash Wednesday?" I ask curiously, in between tasty mouthfuls of my now meat-filled pancake. Something traditional, no doubt...

Josh's eyes widen slightly. "Nothing."

"At all?"

He shakes his head, still looking bemused.

Darryl's eyebrows go up. Oh boy. Dad always planned jobs on the farm so we didn't do heavy work on Ash Wednesday if we could avoid it, so we could fast. But we always had one meal and two snacks. Nothing? Seriously?

"You're only fourteen, though," Josh adds, tossing his pancake without missing a beat, "which is real borderline for manhood so you can eat if you wanna. If that's okay with Darryl."

Darryl nods. Josh is the boss, but Darryl's my big

sis so some things he defers to her. But *this*...My cheeks burn. "I'm not going to eat if you two don't! Though Father Ben said you don't *have* to fast until you're eighteen, right? Darryl's only seventeen, so only Josh *has* to fast 'cos he's nineteen — and even he doesn't have to eat nothing at all!"

"Ain't right to eat on Ash Wednesday," says Josh firmly. "Not if you're young and healthy. But you two are farmers; you can do what farmers do."

"We're hunters at the moment." Darryl sounds stung. "I'll fast like a hunter — unless it isn't safe." She hesitates. "Are you sure you want to do that T. rex nest tomorrow? Why not leave it until the day after, when you won't be hungry?"

Josh shoots us a sidelong glance, eyes crinkling, as he slides his second pancake onto his plate. "If I do it mid-afternoon, I'll only have missed two meals. What's that gonna matter?"

Ugh, hunters. Tough as rex hide. At home on the farm, large, regular meals were such a fixed part of the day. Whereas Josh thinks nothing of missing one because we're too busy or it isn't safe to stop for it.

If we're doing the nest, then one of us has to be on watch all night and most of tomorrow, until finally — if it's safe — Josh will creep up into those crags and sterilize the she-rex's eggs. All without a bite to eat until the following morning. Oh yeah, the next thirty-six hours are going to be super-fun. Though I guess Ash Wednesday isn't about fun, is it?

DARRYL

I guess it's no surprise hunters do a full fast on Ash Wednesday, since they tend to imitate Saint Desmond, the beloved patron saint of all those who live unSPARKed—outside an electric fence—and that's what he did. I've almost finished rereading *The Memoirs of Saint Desmond the Hermit* so that fact is fresh in my mind as I dig into another pancake.

It'll be tough, but I'm determined to do it. I wish Josh wasn't planning to tackle such a risky contract tomorrow, though. We all ought to be at our best for that. Maybe Josh will change his mind.

After two or three meaty pancakes, we switch to sweet ones, piling on sugar and honey and the chocolate sauce Josh has saved untouched in the cupboard since New Year. Kiko gets a few morsels that he shouldn't really have since he doesn't brush his teeth, but never mind. It's only once a year.

Sugar granules ping from Harry's plate, making Josh glance around from his pancake-making, frowning.

"Harry, stop spreading sugar everywhere," I say, "or you'll be deep-cleaning the 'Vi before bed!"

"Do you want that she-rex to make sardines of

us?" adds Josh sharply.

Harry's winter-pale skin goes bright red, and he puts down the sugar shaker. After almost a year in the 'Vi, he's basically internalized the scent procedures, the same as I have, but I guess in all the pancake-making excitement he forgot that he wasn't at home behind the farm's electric fence, where ants are the worst thing sugar is likely to attract.

At home. It barely feels like home anymore. Home is here in the 'Vi, out in the wilderness, with Josh. Sometimes it feels like we've always known him, like we've always been a family, even though we aren't actually related.

Harry's already fetching a cloth; good. We don't want that nesting she-rex popping down this hill, ripping the roof off and eating us up. After guarding those eggs for maybe a month already with little food, she'll be hungry. The 'Vi is raptor and allosaur proof, but armor heavy enough to protect against a rex just isn't practical.

Josh seems slightly on edge, despite the pancake fun. Maybe he doesn't really like the fasting much...no, it isn't that. It's the rex nesting. One of the most dangerous hunter jobs, second only to hunting raptors on foot. His dad *died* rex nesting.

"Oh, and we've got two rex nesting contracts," West told him, last time we met with Josh's 'uncles' for re-supply.

"Give us one, then," Josh said, sounding slightly too casual.

And West hesitated, then did it. Had to treat Josh like a man, 'cos he is, even in city-eyes. But not being prepared to avoid something isn't the same as Josh looking forward to it.

When we're stuffed too full of pancake to eat another bite—Kiko sprawls over my shoulder, snoring softly—Harry pays for his sugary lapse by getting stuck with clean-up, while Josh and I settle down on each side of the table with a hot drink.

Josh leans back in his chair, sipping and staring at the photo frame on the wall. His dad's rosary hangs from it, along with a mysterious blue raptor feather that he still won't explain. The familiar family pictures cycle past—his dad, his uncle, and child-Josh at different ages, with the odd photo of West and the others. He doesn't seem to want to talk, returning brief answers to anything Harry says, so I pick up my handPad. I'm hoping to finish Saint Des's 'Memoirs' tonight, because I want to read *The Imitation of Christ* during Lent, the first proper grown-up book of that kind I'll have tackled.

This last chapter deals with the different theories about how Saint Des survived living in that cave of his for twenty years with no electric fence or armored walls to protect him from predators. A miracle, sure, but how did it work?

Supporters of the Eucharistic miracle theory point to an episode in the life of Saint Clare that tells how, once, a fierce Saracen army invaded San Damiano, entering the very cloister of the virgins. Terrified, the nuns ran to their Mother Superior, Saint Clare, who lay ill in bed.

Fearlessly, she got up and prostrated herself before the Lord. "I pray You, Lord, protect these, Your handmaids, whom I cannot now save by myself."

A voice like that of a little child resounded in her ears from the tabernacle: "I will always protect you!"

So, taking a monstrance of silver and ivory containing the Blessed Sacrament, she confronted the intruders, while her nuns—losing their fear—followed behind. Upon which, quite unaccountably, the Saracens took flight and fled, leaving them all unharmed.

Although the miracle of Saint Clare is categorized as a Eucharistic miracle because of the voice from the tabernacle, it is not clear whether it was the actual presence of Our Lord in the Blessed Sacrament that put the invaders to flight, or the sheer faith of Saint Clare and the nuns, or some other intervention from God. In the same way, we will never know for certain in this life exactly how Saint Desmond lived, preserved from all harm for twenty years amidst fierce predators. But that is all right.

We do not need to know how. Only that he did.

Thanks be to God.

The End.

"I do *like* the Eucharistic theory," I say, putting aside my handPad as Harry finally settles down with his own drink. "You know—that Saint Desmond had a little oratory in the cave with the Blessed Sacrament, and that was what kept the predators away?"

Josh nods, glancing at the gun cabinet, inside which our own little home tabernacle nestles in the carefully converted explosives box. We are *so* blessed—a home tabernacle isn't a right, it's an immense privilege. Farms often have one, but HabVis don't usually—long story.

"Yeah, but he didn't carry Our Lord *around* with him," Josh agrees. "So who knows? I asked Father Ben, and he said that if you left the Blessed Sacrament lying outside most often an animal would simply come along and gobble Him up. When an animal does respond to Him, it sure is a miracle, no question."

He glances from me to the gun cabinet again. Right, he wants Adoration. What did I expect, bringing the subject up? It's Josh's 'Vi, but I'm the only one who has permission from Father Ben to expose the Sacrament, even though all I have to do is turn the knob to open the spiral lattice in the front of the pyx.

"Sure," I say. "When Harry's had his hot chocolate."

Josh gets busy folding the table up out of the way and checking the living area is clean and tidy enough to host a divine Guest. By the time Harry's finished,

Josh has placed two unlit candles ready on each side of the gun cabinet and is eyeing me hopefully again. Josh is really badly catechized, even now, despite my efforts to pass on what I know—but he's always ready for Adoration. He reminds me of that wonderful, loyal dog Uncle Mau had when I was a child. The way it would just gaze at its master, not *understanding*, but loving *so much*. Josh puts me to shame.

When I get up and head for the gun cabinet, Josh and Harry kneel, Harry with only a small, resigned groan.

It is Ash Wednesday tomorrow, after all.

JOSHUA

"Harry, you take the first watch. I'll take the small hours. Darryl, dawn shift."

We've finished Adoration, had another drink, and we're ready to turn in. Harry's face falls and Darryl gives me an anxious look.

"Josh, are you sure we should do this contract tomorrow? Why not start stake-out on Thursday night and do it on Friday?"

It wouldn't be a bad plan but—I just... "We're doing the nest tomorrow." I know I'm coming off as bossier than usual, but I really don't know how to explain why I wanna. Tomorrow is a holy day, and I *need* that ...

Fortunately, they're well-enough trained now to accept that what the boss says goes. Farmers don't argue back quite like city-folk, but they don't always obey quite like born hunters, neither. That settled, we disperse toward our berths—or rather, me toward mine, Darryl toward hers and Harry up the ladder to the observation turret.

+

By the time I take over from a bleary-eyed Harry the moon is out, illuminating the nightscape in a wash of clear light. Not that it matters, with the heat-sensors. But it does make the watch more enjoyable.

I scan the landscape by eye, then check the thermal images on the console screens. I send the drone out as frequently as the battery will allow, monitoring the whole of the surrounding area, going a lot farther out than I usually would.

The maze of boulders ahead blocks us from getting the 'Vi closer than a half-mile to the nest, so we need to be very, very sure there ain't no predators nowhere nearby before I set off. Trouble is, raptors can move real fast and we can check as carefully as we like, it still ain't impossible a pack could show up before I could get back to the 'Vi, especially if there were the slightest delay. And that ain't speculation—I *know*. Sure wish I didn't …

But the nest has to be done. The Dinosaur Activity and Population department want the eggs sterilized,

111

with one left untouched. Time to let a baby rex hatch in this region. The goal is always to have enough rex to keep the herbi'saur population stable, with as few extra juveniles around to blunder through farm—and even city—fences as possible. It sure ain't worth going out there tomorrow for the money—I'll be going out for the farmers, for Darryl and Harry's neighbors and all the others. Even the crazy city-folk.

Usually I like doing a nest where you get to leave an egg. Nice to imagine the she-rex as a proud mother.

I stare up at the dark line of the crags against the night sky. Anger...*hate*...bubbles inside. *This* rex...I'd rather lug my rex gun up there and shoot the creature.

No. *No.* I struggle to let the horrible feelings go, breathing slowly, remembering sitting quietly in the presence of the Lord earlier. I do love having that tabernacle onboard.

The hate—thank God—fades away again, like water flowing downstream. Unfortunately, that leaves nothing to mask the fear, the fear that's had me on edge all evening. Every time I think about going up to that nest tomorrow it coils through my belly, freeze-drying me from the inside out.

It ain't so much fear of dying—first time I truly thought I were about to die I were eleven years old—that's just life, I can deal with *that*. No, it's the fear that when it's actually time to get out of the 'Vi and head up that hillside, I simply won't be able to do it. That the past will overwhelm me and I'll freeze. That the fear will win.

Saint Des, please help me.

Lord, give me courage.

'Cos that...that would be worse than dying. To lose myself like that. To lose *to* myself.

No, the nest has to be done. And I'm gonna do it.

DARRYL

The dawn light bounces off the mist, touching the rocky slopes with gold. It's harder to appreciate the beauty with my eyelids this heavy—usually I'm just getting up about now. Tired or not, I should enjoy the greenery while I can. We'll be heading back to the high snowy mountains as soon as we've completed this contract.

Josh and Harry are sleeping in, no surprise. I scan the landscape, then check the thermal imaging carefully. No sign of any carni'saurs. Time to launch the drone again.

Kiko lands in my lap, seeking attention, but I don't let him distract me. Later on today, Josh's life may depend on how well we keep watch.

It isn't much longer before slight movements of the vehicle tell me that Josh is up. He's always awake before Harry. Usually before me.

Soon the hatch opens and his head appears, dark

hair and terracotta skin damp from the shower. He settles in another seat, leaving the hatch open, of course, since it's just the two of us, and offers me a mug. I accept it and sip eagerly, though it's only boiled water. After sitting up here for hours, the night chill is getting to me, even in this milder region.

Josh stares up toward the crags as he sips his steaming water, his expression bleak. Has he done a rex nest since his dad died? I'm sure he talked about doing some with his Uncle Z. It seems to be a point of pride among hunter-borns that each HabVi does one or two nests each spring.

Despite the danger.

Finally, Josh gives his head a slight shake and turns his chair around, putting his back to the nest. "Any activity?"

I shake my head. "It's quiet. There are various herbi'saurs around. I kept a record, but if you stay alert and don't walk into them, nothing dangerous."

"Good."

HARRY

Hot water for breakfast. Nothing else. Then Josh burns a little pile of dried willow clippings up in the turret and mixes the ash with some Holy Water, reciting several hunter prayers seeking Saint Des's intercession for a safe and holy Lent.

He ends up with a pot of soggy ashes not unlike the ones Father Ben gives each household shortly before Lent—though I think Father Ben makes his out of old palm crosses. Occasionally he's even at the farm on Ash Wednesday to administer them himself, but a rural priest can't be everywhere.

As the eldest, Josh stands in for Father Ben, the way Dad always did, carefully marking a cross on my forehead—"Remember you are dust, and to dust you shall return"—then on Darryl's. "Remember you are dust, and to dust you shall return."

For once, it doesn't make me want to giggle, everyone getting smeared with ashes. Today, out in the wilds, it feels really...real. What Josh is going to do later is dangerous, and there's no getting around that.

"Harry, you're the youngest." Josh offers me the pot.

Oh, do I have to do him? I take the pot and dip my finger—he bends his neck. I wipe the ash onto his forehead, trying to make a neat cross. "Uh...remember you are dust, and...to dust you shall return..." Annoyingly, my voice vibrates slightly, but Josh just smiles a thank you and takes the pot back.

No doubt there's a tradition for disposing of what's left!

JOSHUA

It's mid-afternoon. Almost time to make my move.

My heart's pounding in my chest.

I've gone over and over each scenario with Darryl and Harry, since they've never rex-nested before. They only need to fly the drone and lure the rex away and, above all, keep lookout. I trust 'em to do it. It ain't them I don't trust today.

Sweat trickles down my spine.

All three of us have stayed on watch for most of the day and we ain't seen no carni'saurs. No need to postpone. Part of me's disappointed, but part of me's glad. If I'm finding it this hard, even on this special holy day, how much worse will it be tomorrow?

I make one last check and force myself to stand. "Right." Ugh, my voice sounds like Harry's when he were ashing my forehead. I strengthen it, sounding too loud instead. "I'm gonna go below, get ready. Darryl, come down in a minute and collect the meat for the bait. Put Kiko in the critter cage—no distractions."

I slide down the ladder and move to the table, where my rex-nesting backpack sits—Uncle Z's, it were before—with its proper silent-release buckles. Not a scrap of Velcro, no zips, nothing to clink or clank and draw eight tons of motherly wrath with a mouthful of ten-inch teeth.

Opening it, I check the contents, though I only packed it earlier.

In my head, I hear my own voice, younger, higher pitched:

"Can't I do it? I'm fourteen now. I've done several rex nests already. Don't I need the practice?"

Sterilization fluid. Syringe. Odor neutralizer. Check...

And Dad's voice:

"Not this nest, Josh. You're not doing this nest, not while your Uncle Z or I are around to do it."

They ain't around to do it...no more. I'm the oldest and most experienced. I have to do it. Though I no longer wanna.

Oh, why did West give me this nest?

Please, Saint Des, give me strength!

DARRYL

When I slide down the ladder with Kiko on my shoulder, Josh is carefully applying scentBlock cream, pushing up his sleeves to do well above his elbows and smearing it down under his shirt at the neck. His hands shake slightly. I thought the only thing that bothered him this much was going in-city.

The cream is mottled brown-green for extra camouflage, which the now-smeared ashes on his forehead only help with, though Josh's darker skin always gives him an advantage over Harry or myself— except in snow.

I shut Kiko into the cage. "Josh?"

"Everything's ready." He grabs the little pack and swings it onto his back.

"Josh, are you okay?"

"I'm fine."

He steps toward the side door—but when he gets there he places his palms against it, leaning over, staring at the floor, breathing hard. Still shaking.

The possibility of being eaten is ever-present for a hunter, but it's never seemed to faze him. *Why* is this different, here, today? Is it just because it's a rex nest, and that's how his dad died?

Or is it... Oh, no, surely not!

"Josh, is *this* where your dad died?"

JOSHUA

When I don't reply, Darryl grabs my arm, pulling me around to face her. "Oh, Josh, it *isn't*, is it?"

I nod without speaking. My gaze rests on the floor beside the door—for a moment I'm down there, wrestling with Uncle Z as he tries to stop me from rushing out to help Dad—'cos it's too late.

"Josh! You don't have to do this nest!" Darryl's fierce voice breaks in on the memory. "You don't! *Ever.*"

"The nest needs doing, and we got the contract." My voice comes out tight and flat. "So I do."

"No! *How* could West give you this nest?"

"He didn't know!" I snap, hating hearing my own accusation coming from her mouth. "He had two rex nesting contracts, and he simply gave me one. *I didn't* even open the file until later that day. Why would he? There's a lotta rex nests in this state!"

"You don't have to do it, Josh! Look, I'll...*I'll* go do it!"

"No. Absolutely no *short-circuiting* way!" I'm wearing a throat mike, and I lower my voice to double-check it's working. "Harry, all clear?"

"Y-yes?" Clearly he's heard what we've been saying.

"Good. I'm going. Darryl, be ready to lure the she-rex away."

"Josh—!"

I feel one hair from sitting down in the corner and sobbing and never moving again; the only thing that might get me out of this vehicle is the thought of her going up to that nest instead of me. *Yeah, that works...*

I hit the door's "open" button and leap to the ground.

"Josh!"

Letting it slide closed behind me, I set off up the hillside at more of a blind sprint than a jog.

No, calm down, Josh. You're out-'Vi. Get it together.

I pause behind a large boulder and draw in deep breaths, fighting for control.

"Josh, you okay?" Darryl's voice comes through my earpiece.

"Fine."

"Please come back." Her voice catches slightly. "You shouldn't have to do this."

"Shouldn't? What the heck does that even mean? It's a rex nest that needs doing, and that's all there is to it. We've done everything just the way we should. It'll be *fine*."

I turn and move up the slope again, at a gentle jog this time, watching for danger.

Harry's nervous voice comes from my earpiece. "But I thought your *dad* did everything just the way — *ooph*." He breaks off as though his breath has been driven from him by a sisterly elbow.

Yeah, thanks, Harry. Dad did *do everything just right, but that ain't really the most helpful thing to hear right now.*

Or mebbe it is. Dad did everything just right and he still got et up, which means it were his time. And if it's your time, it's your time. What am I worrying about? I just have to do my part the very best I can and the rest is up to God and Saint Des. *Yeah, stop being an idiot, Josh.*

I keep moving, nice and steady. My hands have finally stopped shaking. Good. I guess making it out of the 'Vi were the hard part.

"Darryl," I say, as I get higher up the slope, almost

out of their sight. "Start luring the rex away. Going silent now. Don't speak to me unless it's critical."

HARRY

Darryl pilots the drone with a chunk of meat dangling from a strong spiderline, while I maintain watch. It takes a huge effort to keep my eyes on my task and not glance at the drone screen to see what's happening. Without the drone, my field of vision is vastly reduced.

Darryl clearly appreciates how much of a struggle it is because—our mics carefully muted—she keeps me up to date.

"Okay, the she-rex has smelled the meat. She's getting up. Yep, she's following the drone. I'm trying to catch the meat between the two rocks Josh picked out. Almost...okay, the meat's off the line. She's maneuvering toward it, but not too fast..."

JOSHUA

By the time I reach the nest hollow, the she-rex is moving away, her featherless hide rippling as she stomps along. She-rex barely eat for three months while guarding their nests—she ain't gonna turn down a tempting morsel she can snatch quickly.

Okay, she's far enough out of earshot. I creep

down into the hollow, placing my steps with great care. If I knock two rocks together, she'll be back faster than you can say "RIP Josh."

Here's the nest, a well-built, hard-packed mound. I inspect the eggs quickly. Four. Okay, this one looks the very best—large, strong, with good color. Rex Junior. Opening my backpack, I swiftly inject sterilization fluid into the other three, spray the nest with odor neutralizer—though this rex probably associates human scent with a tasty snack—and begin creeping back up the slope.

I've been real quick. That's good.

But I'm only half-way when Darryl speaks softly—and tensely—from my earpiece. "Rex on her way back."

Already? I move as fast as I possibly can, step by careful step. Heck, I chose a position for the meat much further away than last time. And she still got it too soon. Clever girl.

Heavy footfalls from the entrance gully... My heart's pounding but I keep moving, careful, careful...

The lip of the hollow looms ahead. Nearly there. Nearly...

"Josh, freeze!"

Misfire! I drop gently onto my belly on the slope and lie motionless, clinging tightly to my calm. It's okay. They know what to do. Just call the drone back, re-bait it, and lure the rex away again. And I lie nice and still here and try not to take a nap.

Nap, yeah right. This is *exactly* what happened to Dad. The rex coming back too soon...

Yeah, but that weren't why she *caught* him. She only caught him 'cos the approaching Utahraptors forced him to make a run for it. So I'm *fine*. I just lie here quietly until the rex leaves again. So long as I don't move, I'm just a boulder to the she-rex.

DARRYL

My heart pounds wildly. With the drone on route back to the turret, Harry and I can't see Josh anymore, and that's almost unbearable. We just have to trust he's okay. "Josh would never move an inch near a rex, Harry," I say, though my voice sounds strangled. "You know that. He'll be fine. Just keep watch."

Pale-faced, Harry obeys.

Ugh, come on, drone, come on!

I've got the drone on the fastest setting, but a glimpse of something on the screen and I bring it quickly to a halt, zooming in one of the cameras.

A wave of coldness washes from my head to my toes.

No!

JOSHUA

Darryl's voice comes very, very softly, 'cos she knows the rex is in the hollow with me—in fact, the rex-mom is relaxing at the bottom of the slope, lying slightly on her side, huge head stretched out as she enjoys a ray of sun.

"Dakotaraptors coming from the north. About four minutes until they cut you off."

I squeeze my eyes closed, my cheek pressed to the rock, fighting, fighting to keep breathing ever so slow and steady and inconspicuous, fighting to keep hold of myself so I don't start to shake visibly.

This is exactly what happened to Dad.

Different species of raptor—brown instead of grey and a foot shorter, a little lighter, much difference that will make. *Saint Des, help!*

"Josh, what do we do?" Darryl's still speaking very softly, her voice shaky. 'Cos I ain't given 'em instructions for this scenario. There ain't nothing they *can* do.

Just audibly, I breathe, "Stay in the 'Vi. It'll be fine."

Liar. But what can I say? I've the same choice Dad had. Lie still and let the raptors cut me off from the 'Vi—almost certain death—or make a run for that lip right away and hope the rex lets me go if I make it over—very probable death.

But number two, beat the raptors back to the 'Vi...it's now or never.

DARRYL

I cut our mikes again, staring at the drone screen, where one camera now shows Josh, flat on that slope, while the other shows the rapidly approaching Dakotaraptor pack.

Fine?

"Liar, Josh!" I whisper, my hands clenched so tight they hurt. What to *do*? He's going to die, just the way his dad died!

"Darryl?" stammers Harry.

Josh thinks there's nothing we *can* do, that's clear enough. I mean, if the raptors come close enough, we could shoot at them, hope it sends them off in a different direction. But they look more on a trajectory for the rex nest. Are they hungry enough after the winter to try to steal her eggs? It's a large pack, ten adults and no fewer than five juveniles, their plumage many shades of Dakotaraptor-brown. Yeah, they're going for the nest, aren't they? And they're not going to come within range of our rifles. Curse this terrain! We can barely move the HabVi around on it at all, most directions blocked by huge boulders.

"Darryl?" Harry practically sobs the word. "We've *got to help him!"*

JOSHUA

I've been raised to be real decisive in a crisis, yet now I lie motionless, racked with indecision. *Weigh the odds...*

The odds say I make a run for it, like Dad did—but I know too well how it will end.

What will Darryl and Harry do? Oh, please God, let them stay inside! If they try to come help me, to attempt to drive the pack off...

Heck, if I get one hint of that, I'm gonna jump up right away; take my chances with the rex. Two rifles ain't enough to fend off a whole pack of Dakotaraptors. They've *gotta* stay safe in the 'Vi!

DARRYL

Saint Des, help!

Lord...

Panicking, drowning in helpless desperation, I slide down the ladder and throw myself to my knees in front of the gun cabinet, my forehead pressing against the cold metal. *Lord, please, oh, please! How can I save Josh? How?*

Deep down inside me, a little voice whispers that I can't. I simply *can't.*

I'm quivering on the point of total break-down when another little voice, that isn't quite like my own little voice, says: *But I can.*

I can.

I...

My brain thrumming with white-out hope, I leap to my feet and dive for the main console. Tapping quickly, I cut off Harry's communication with Josh, then type in a code Josh shared with me that will stop the doors being opened from the inside after they're next closed, until the override is input.

"Darryl, what do we *do*?"

Ignoring Harry's wail from the turret, I hurtle back to the gun cabinet, place my hand on the scanner, wait, then yank the door open. I genuflect, then place my hand on the scanner again to open the inner explosives-box-tabernacle, waiting impatiently. *Come on, come on...*

A year later, the lock clicks. I swing the door open, dip down to the floor and up again, then move aside the shimmering feather-fabric curtain with a trembling hand. There's the pyx, the size of my palm, covered by its lace veil. Drawing the veil off, I carefully pick it up, turning the knob at the back to open the lattice, and move toward the door.

I pause for a moment, drawing a deep breath. But...

I can.

HE *can*. The certainty that floods me is...absolute. Complete. Indescribable. I take one hand from the pyx and open the door, then climb carefully down to the ground.

"Darryl? What the heck are you —?" The closing door

cuts off Harry's panic-stricken words as his head pops down through the turret hatch. *Sorry, Harry.*

Holding the pyx before me, I head steadily up the slope. Less than half a mile, an easy walk on the grass winding between the outcrops. Five to ten minutes to reach Josh?

"Okay, Josh," I speak very softly, "looking at your position right now, the very best thing you can do is stay still and wait, okay? Don't reply, don't make any noise. Just wait. I'll tell you when it's safe to move."

Considering the she-rex is resting comfortably right beside her nest, teeth bare yards from his heels, Josh must be puzzled by the idea that he should soon move. But he stays silent. Waiting? Good.

Because another thing I'm sure of: if Josh knows I'm out here, he'll feed himself to the rex at once if it will get me back inside the 'Vi faster.

HARRY

My mind spins, terror trying to overwhelm me. Josh is trapped in a rex nest and Darryl... Darryl is walking calmly up the slope holding the pyx out in front of her like she's taking part in some kind of...solemn procession. She's going to get eaten! They're *both* going to get eaten and there's nothing I can do!

"Josh, Darryl's out-'Vi; do something!" But how can he help her when he's stuck himself? "*Josh?*"

He doesn't answer. Is he ignoring me? He wouldn't ignore *that*. I check the console. My mike is muted. I try to turn it back on, but I can't. From that little symbol on the screen, the doors are locked, too. How did Darryl do that?

Movement on the screens... Oh no, the raptors have scented Darryl! She's not wearing any scentBlock. They're flowing toward her...

I yank the lever to raise the windows and position my rifle's tip through the bars...but they're too far up the slope. A few glimpses of feathery tails behind distant boulders, nothing more. I glance at the screen again, at the drone camera's view from above, my insides clenching up—

Darryl keeps walking right toward them. Has she lost her mind? They cock their heads, eyeing her, colorful ruffs flaring around their leathery faces. They dart back a few massive, bouncing, yards-long strides—Dakotaraptors are big, man-high, taller than Darryl. Then they cock their heads to inspect her again.

Again, they dart away, killing claws held clear of the ground. Why are they running? Is it her they're looking at—or the pyx?

Whichever, they keep moving away and she simply keeps walking, with reverent steps, through the Dakotaraptors and up toward that rex nest...

JOSHUA

"Okay, Josh." Darryl's voice again, still so calm that there must be some hope. Have the raptors moved away? Are they about to lure the rex again? "I'm here. Just get up and walk slowly to me."

What? Fear closes around my throat like a raptor's jaws, my eyes jerking upward, my head turning slightly before I can stop it.

She *is* here. Literally, *here*. Standing right on the rim of the hollow, holding...holding the *pyx*? The pale golden circle of Our Lord's Body shows behind the open lattice.

What the—?

My eyes dart down into the hollow as the she-rex moves, rolling, getting her feet under her. But she stays sitting, staring up at Darryl, at Him, her bushy reddish-brown crest feathers rising.

"Lord," Darryl speaks clearly in a gentle, soothing tone appropriate for an anxious mother, "please bless this she-rex and her un-hatched chick. *Come on, Josh. Please* grant them health and long life and plentiful prey..."

Oooookay, the rex still ain't attacking. Slowly, carefully, I ease to my feet and begin to move up the slope, resuming the chaplet of Saint Desmond I were partway through.

Jesus, I trust in You...

Jesus, I trust in You...

The mother rex carries on staring at Darryl. Or mebbe at Him.

"Lord, please keep them away from fences and from all conflict with humans. Please don't let them ever eat anyone or need to be shot."

No one *else*. Softly, softly, I pick my way upwards, step by step.

"And we pray, Lord, for the repose of Isaiah Wilson and beg your blessing on his son, Joshua..."

I swallow a lump in my throat. I'm literally walking over the exact spot where those motherly teeth sank into Dad...

"Lord, please bless this she-rex with mild winters and gentle summers... *Come on, Josh...*"

I creep faster, afraid to make sudden moves, but also fearful Darryl's inventiveness will run out and the blessing end before I get up there. Irrational, 'cos it sure ain't *Darryl* that's keeping that rex sitting there...

"Lord, may this nest be a safe place for this mother. May no raptors steal her eggs or harm her chick."

And I'm stepping up onto the rim of the hollow beside her, staring down at the she-rex.

"Amen," Darryl finishes.

Despite everything, I have a moment of silent struggle with myself. I don't wanna hate nothing, even this she-rex... "Amen," I whisper, adding my blessing to Darryl's—then I step slowly backward when she does.

"Just...stay behind me," says Darryl, as she turns around to face downslope.

"What—? *Oh...*" *Great.*

Dakotaraptors. A large pack, spread across the hillside, watching us. Darryl starts toward 'em, calm as anything. I guess she walked through 'em to get up here, right? After what just happened at the rex nest... I take hold of the hem of her jacket and follow close behind.

Is this all a strange dream? I feel awake. Uncle Z told me how he went berserk, once, under extreme stress. Ran at a pack of Dakotaraptors, single-handed, just him and his rifle, screaming like a lunatic. Chased 'em off. Has Darryl gone berserk? Like, spiritually? There's probably a special word for it.

Our Lord is obviously smiling on us right now, anyway. A big, beaming, luminous smile, bathing us in this inexplicable protection. It's beautiful. I just wanna enjoy the moment. Try not to be scared…

Darryl is watching her footing too carefully to pray for the raptors, so I recite Saint Des's 'Blessing Over a Sick Carni'saur' as we walk. Okay, they quite definitely ain't sick—sleek feathers and rippling muscles—but I ain't feeling too inventive. The raptors follow us the whole way, peering curiously, whisking away, peering again, in that way they do when they ain't sure about something.

Soon—incredibly—we're coming into sight of the

'Vi, where a lonely figure stands in the turret, rifle raised.

"Harry," I say softly, "hold your fire."

This is a miracle. Has to be.

So nothing needs to die today.

DARRYL

Josh types in the override code to open the doors while I stand, still holding up the pyx as though inviting the raptors to adore Him. They keep staring, though I'm not sure if they're worshipping or just trying to figure Him out or simply not being allowed to attack us, somehow.

Despite the unearthly sense of confidence that I've floated in since that little not-Darryl voice spoke inside me, the sound of the sliding door hissing back has rarely been so welcome. Josh grips my waist, steadying me and boosting me as I place one heel into the foothold and climb up backwards, keeping Our Lord pointed toward the raptors.

Josh rolls in after me and hits the door's "close" button.

Hiss. Click.

Safe. My legs sag as the reality of what I just did hits. Josh catches me and lowers me to my knees. "Darryl? You okay?"

Nodding, I clutch the pyx to my chest in a rather

unorthodox fashion because my arms are shaking so much that I'm afraid I'll drop it. Huh, what will Father Ben say about me taking it out there like that? I hope that was okay.

Then Harry's down the ladder, throwing himself on us and enfolding us in a tight hug, sobbing hysterically. Josh wraps his arms around us too, and Our Lord ends up squashed in the middle of the hug, but it's hard to believe He minds, there's so much love in it.

"I thought you were gonna die," Harry gasps, once we're all smeared with ashes and scentBlocker and sweat and tears and probably some snot. "*I thought you were both gonna die!*"

"I'm sorry, Harry," I whisper. "I didn't have time to explain."

"Explain what?"

"That it was going to be okay."

"How could you know that?"

I hesitate. Here's where I'm going to sound like a crazy person. I'm limp and shaking now, but I still remember that absolute certainty... "I was thinking how I couldn't save Josh and a voice inside me that wasn't me—I think it was Our Lord—said... well, communicated, that *He* could. That's why I took the pyx."

"A voice you thought was God said He could save Josh so you *took the pyx and climbed out of the 'Vi?*"

Harry's voice rises incredulously as Josh listens silently.

"Uh, yeah?"

"But when God says things like that it usually means, like, *don't worry that Josh is going to get eaten because I'll save him spiritually*—his *soul*, right? Didn't it even *cross your mind* that's what it meant?"

I pause, my mouth hanging open. "No," I say at last. "No, that wasn't how I took it."

"Perfect faith," murmurs Josh. "Like Saint Des. That's why God honored it. Whether you misunderstood or not."

Okay, this conversation is getting *way* embarrassing. Since when do I have *perfect faith*, like Saint Des? What I just experienced...that was a gift from God, it wasn't *me*. This is total speculation, anyway.

"Look, I need to put the pyx away..." I raise it with shaking hands. Josh takes my wrist, steadying it, then leans in and touches his lips to the glass and I've never seen a kiss more sincere.

"Thank You," he whispers.

Yeah, I know how he feels. I kiss the pyx too. *"Thank You."*

Shaking, wild-eyed, Harry leans in as well and kisses it without a trace of embarrassment. "Thank You!"

I stand, wobbly-legged, long enough to return the pyx to its secure home, then sink down on the floor again. Harry remains slumped nearby.

"That...that was a miracle, right?" he whispers. Looking at Josh, the resident animal behavioral expert.

Josh smiles, his eyes bright, his expression radiantly dazed. "Sure were."

"Is anyone ever going to believe us?"

"Nope," says Josh. "We can tell Father Ben. But there ain't much point in telling no one else about something like this—unless he wants us too." He glances up at his blue feather. "Trust me on that."

HARRY

We sit in silence for a while, until my stomach gives a mighty gurgle. "I am *so* hungry," I groan.

Josh and Darryl open their mouths—I scowl, cheeks hot, wishing I'd kept quiet. "*No!* I am *not* eating anything after God just *saved* you two like that. Forget it! Not *one bite* until midnight."

Darryl laughs so hard she holds her sides, and so does Josh.

"*What?*"

"Sorry, just picturing you hovering beside the fridge at one minute to midnight, waiting."

"Yeah," smirks Josh. "'Cos I promise you, *I* shall be asleep in bed."

I have to grin, too. "Oh. Yeah. Guess I will be too. We are allowed breakfast tomorrow, right?"

Josh nods. "Sure. Oatmeal. With the last of the ashes in it."

The ashes. We're going to *eat* them. Of course we are.

Welcome to Lent, hunter-style.

For some reason, I'm becoming increasingly sure I want to be a farmer. Unlike my big sis.

But we're all *alive*. Yeah, after today, nothing a hunter-Lent can throw at me is gonna make me waver. Grumble a little, probably—but not waver.

Thank you, God!

UNSPARKED
A VERY
JURASSIC
CHRISTMAS
CORINNA TURNER
CARNEGIE MEDAL NOMINEE

CHRISTMAS EVE

JOSHUA

Skating gently across the frozen lake, keeping my speed in check, I ready myself—and execute a little spin. Without falling on my rear. Yes!

I'm improving, but progress is slow, because I get only a few days to skate each year. Dad and Uncle Z drove north far into the wilds of Tana State for a Christmas break every year since I was seven, just so that I could skate out in the open countryside instead of inside one of the looming, crowded urban rinks further south. Those invariably sent city-phobic me— wilderness-raised boy that I am—into a panic.

What was it like in the old days, before the crazy scientists and their arrogant assumption that they could contain the creatures they'd bred? Hard to imagine, and I don't waste time trying. So what if the world outside the fenced cities is harsher and more dangerous than it once was? It's my home, and I like it as it is.

Ecstatic at my achievement, I spin again— successfully!—and tear off down the center of the lake, gathering speed. I love the feeling of flying over the ice, so fast, so free. Out here on my skates, I could outrun even a raptor.

Of course, the rest of the pack would box me in fast enough, which is why the biggest Christmas gift Dad and Uncle Z gave me, year after year, wasn't the fuel, but their time, as they sat up there in the Habitat Vehicle's turret, getting anything but a holiday themselves as they kept watch over me. It was always just the three of us in our HabVi, my whole life—no relatives to visit—so we could spend Christmas wherever we wanted. Uncle Z's up in the HabVi's turret now, carrying on the tradition. Only one pair of eyes, the last two years, but that's how it is now.

Pushing away the sadness that twists in my stomach at the thought of Dad, I bend my knees and pile on the speed even more, my heart pounding with healthy effort. I'm sixteen now, and after nine years I can stay up on my feet real well, but I'm only just getting to grips with the fancy maneuvers. I'm certainly not gonna try to spin going at this speed!

The icy wind whips in my face, fluttering my coal-black hair against my forehead, though I always cut it before it's long enough to get in my eyes and block my gun sight. Yes! This is the life. Okay, so I prefer the milder climate of Exception State, really. But I do so love to skate.

"No closer to the far shore, Josh." Uncle Z's voice startles me, coming from my earpiece.

I raise my head, my concentration broken,

wobbling slightly as my eyes scan the snow-blanketed bushes, slopes, and beach coming up ahead.

"Whoa!" I jam my right skate in front of my left one, bringing myself to a rapid halt, heart pounding even harder.

Emerging from the nearest undergrowth is a...yes, a fully grown female allosaur, thirty feet long with a mouth full of razor-sharp four-inch teeth. Uncle Z laughs his head off in my ear, entertained by my emergency stop. He let me get nice and close on purpose, didn't he?

"Very funny, Uncle Z! Aren't you supposed to be on watch?"

"I'm keeping watch better than you, dreamer boy," comes the chortling reply. "Well, she's a skinny, mangy old creature, ripe for culling, doncha think? Let's not look a Christmas gift in the mouth. Bounty on an allo will pay for some of that fuel we burned coming all the way up here."

I eye the huge predator. Same upright conformation as a raptor or T. rex, though far bigger than the largest raptor species and significantly smaller than a T. rex. Resembling a rex more than a feathery raptor with her bare, leathery hide, only a crest of display feathers tops her head. She's thin all right, her ribs showing starkly, but I'm close enough to see that she's *not* old. Or mangy. Just starving. Why? She's moving well enough, and there's no wound that I can see.

She stops at the edge of the frozen lake, stretching her head toward me, nostrils flaring. Close to drooling. Oh yeah, she's hungry.

She actually raises one big clawed foot and places it tentatively on the lake, then draws it back as a creaking boom sounds from the ice. I'm perfectly safe. She's far too heavy to venture out here. She stretches her neck, shuffling her feet, never taking her eyes from me. Having a meal so close is torture.

"Ah, I'll put her out of her misery for you," says Uncle Z. "Stand still until I give you the all clear."

I hear the *chink* of Uncle Z's rifle touching the bars around the turret as he makes sure the muzzle is unimpeded, then the snap of his safety catch coming off. My earpiece will filter out the volume of the shot, so I need only stand and wait.

Something moves in the bushes behind the hungry allosaur. What the...? Surely it can't be...?

But it is!

My hand flies up, palm flat. "Stop, Uncle Z!"

"What's wrong?"

"Look. Coming out of the bushes..."

They're fully visible as they toddle down the beach, one, two, three of them, clustering around the female's stocky legs.

Allosaur chicks. The female is a hungry mom.

DARRYL

"How are things going, Darryl, my girl?" calls Dad as I approach the family room.

"Things are as ready in the kitchen as I can make them," I tell him as I enter, wiping my hands dry on my jeans before reaching up to re-tie my shoulder-length brown hair. "Soon as people begin arriving, we can start warming the cider. Half an hour before, we can slide the pecan pies into the oven. I put the cream in the jugs already and the plates are stacked, everything's sorted."

"Good job. Can you help Harry with the chairs while I go drive the fence early?"

Yeah, I was expecting he'd do it now. He won't want to later, and it's better to check it before we have a load of extra people on the farm for the evening. "Sure, Dad." But my heart sinks. I was kinda hoping that with the catering all ready I could go drive the fence with him, have a few minutes off. I love when it's our turn hosting the Christmas Eve carol service, no mistake, but I've been on my feet working from dawn until...well, it's not dusk yet, but the sun's certainly dropping in the sky. "Is Father Ben here yet?"

"No, not yet."

"I thought he said he'd be here mid-afternoon."

Dad shrugs. "He sent a heads-up when he left as usual—taking the mountain road—but he's running late. He should've come over the last pass half an hour or so ago, so he'll be here any time."

Distress signals rarely make it to the satellite from that winding minor road through the towering mountains that split Exception State in half, and the timid or less experienced driver will invariably drive all the way around on one of the main highways. But it's a really significant shortcut so Father Benedict, being neither timid nor inexperienced and with four-wheel drive, invariably heads straight up and over.

Since it's actually only a carol service tonight, not Mass, Father Benedict's kinda optional, but he'll preach a good homily, and he sings nice and loud. Some folks, like Dad's childhood friend, our neighbor Maurice Carr—who claims he only comes for the refreshments—aren't that enthusiastic at belting out the carols.

My insides clench at the thought of the Carr family. Maurice's wife, Sarah Carr, is really sick and won't be coming tonight. But she's insisting that Uncle Mau bring the children, just as usual. It's no secret, though, that all four Carr children will be as motherless as Harry and I, within a few months. Which is worse, knowing it's coming or having your mother snatched from you in an instant in some stupid farm accident? I shake my head. There's no good way to lose your mom, especially when very young.

"Right, I'm fence-bound." Dad traipses towards the front door, passing my younger brother, Harry, who's staggering under an armful of the folding chairs we use for Sunday Mass. We don't really have any relatives, so other than the carol service and Mass on Christmas morning, we'll have a nice quiet Christmas with just the three of us and Father Ben, though he can only stay until lunch on Saint Stephen's Day.

I head to the hall cupboard to fetch more chairs. It's the only event of the year when we need every last one. Just as I reach the cupboard, Harry darts past and gets inside ahead of me.

"Hey, I was here first! You can't have set up those last chairs yet!" I try to pull him out—he resists. "Don't be so— Let *me*—"

He grabs hold of another stack of chairs, so that I drag him and the stack out into the hall together, screeching noisily over the wooden floor.

"Darryl, are you fourteen or four?" Dad's poised to exit the house, giving me a look over his shoulder.

"Harry started it!"

"Harry's eleven. You're not. 'Nough said." He steps out and the door closes behind him.

Red-faced, I release Harry. Why did I let his childish behavior get to me? Especially when Dad was *right there.*

"Fine, take them," I tell Harry, who's biting his lip, embarrassed too.

He musters an unconvincing smirk, making out that getting his own way was worth Dad saying he was just a little kid, and staggers off with them.

By the time I return with my own stack he's setting out chairs as though he's forgotten all about it. He pauses to push his short brown hair behind his winter-pale ears with both hands and say, "I wonder why Father Ben's so late."

"Something came up, I guess. Well, he'll be here any minute. Let's finish this and get our afternoon chores done."

Soon enough we've squeezed all the seats we can into the family room, spilling out into the doorways to the hall and dining room, and we're putting the finishing touches to the decorations.

"There." I straighten a big red bow on the front door and put my hands on my hips with a satisfied nod. The farmhouse's steel shutters are all open, proclaiming the efficiency of our twin Renfield Ozone 4 electric fence, and Dad's even circled the turret on top of the house with little fairy lights. Harry, having arranged a cheerful Christmas hat on the head of the little statue of Saint Desmond on one side of the door, is carefully draping the dainty, red velvet cloak that Mom made years ago around the Our Lady statue opposite. "I think we're ready. Let's get the chores done, then we can shower and change and hang out with Father Ben when he arrives."

"Okey-dokey." Harry bounces off toward the barn.

"Don't forget to check on that sick edmontosaur in the handling barn," I call after him.

Although I'm outside already, I reflexively check my ScreamerBand—no alarms have been tripped, the fence remains unbreached and secure—then head to the young stock barn.

Soon, I'm dropping the calf feeder over the side of the bovine pen. I give only a few quick scratches to the eager butting heads as they crowd forward to drink, then trundle the much bigger "milk" trolley along to the other, larger half of the barn, where the 'saur calves are kept carefully separate from their fragile mammalian bottle mates.

Plugging the pump tube into the milk trolley—which actually contains green liquid feed mix, but it's the same consistency as milk so we tend to call it that—I switch it on, then lean over the fence, looking down into the pen—the floor is lowered, of course, like all 'saur handling pens—or rather, the obsoDeck is raised—though here the concrete walls drop only six foot.

"Dinner, y'all," I call. A pair of two-month-old male edmo calves and a single female iggy calf, all three already as tall as I am and weighing five times as much, lumber up to the feeder. The "original" 'saurs didn't grow as fast as ours do now, so they reckon, but the scientists didn't think their buyers would want to wait around. Sure suits us farmers.

The edmos latch onto a teat each, while Janey the

iggy raises her flat head level with me, her beaky mouth parted hopefully.

"Just a quick scratch," I tell her, obliging. "I've got to hurry!"

I rub the itchy spot behind her jaw for a few moments. "Okay, enough, Janey. Go have your milk."

I've no bovine calves left to individually feed, but one runty little iguanodon is still on the bottle. I move to the end pen and let myself in, clucking encourage-ingly until the gangly little male iggy gets to his feet and totters forward as I step inside the safety ring. Only coming up to my chest and being very weak, it's still safe to come in here with him. A bigger calf could crush this little metal rail just by leaning on it too hard.

"Good boy." I offer him the bottle, and he takes the teat readily. He can graduate to the feeder soon. I don't scratch him as he feeds, except for massaging his chin to encourage him to start sucking again when he loses interest. It's not a good idea to make pets of male stock. The few top quality males we keep as stud animals are always sold to other farms, with only good, sound females remaining here as breeding stock. Janey is in with a good chance of staying, if she carries on growing so well.

Soon, he's emptied his bottle and, after checking him over, I'm collecting the empty milk trolley and calf feeder and heading back to the mix room to wash everything. I'll feed my charges again just before bed —

probably with a gaggle of hyper younger guests trailing after me, tonight—and again first thing in the morning, Christmas Day or not.

Reaching the farmhouse again, I eye the empty yard and frown, my stomach chilling. Still no Father Benedict. Where is he? I check the time on my ScreamerBand. Only an hour until the service is supposed to begin and well over an hour since Dad said he'd arrive any minute. Heading inside, I'm checking the House Control console for messages when I hear Dad's farm truck stop in front of the house. He's done with the fence.

"Anything?"

I glance over my shoulder, shaking my head, as Dad strides into the house. "Nothing. Just his heads-up message from earlier."

Dad's mouth tightens, and he raises his ScreamerBand to his mouth, pressing the talk button. "Harry, get back here and grab your rifle. We're going to find Father Ben."

He lowers his wrist and glances at me. "Darryl, start the..." He hesitates, and I can guess what he's thinking. The hunting truck has a rudimentary turret, allowing better defense, but the normal road truck has stronger towing capabilities. Father Benedict's van is a heftier vehicle than some mere car, and there's little doubt now that he's stopped somewhere in the mountains. *Broken down* being the far preferable scenario than *crashed*, though both are extremely dangerous.

Dad makes a face. "Start the road truck, I guess."

Yeah, neither vehicle is perfect for this.

"And do the safety checks," he adds.

Okay, he's really worried if he's going to trust me to check the grilles and wheel shields so we can get away quicker. Dad always does the checks himself.

As I place a hand on the scanner of the gun locker, he presses the "record" button on the console and starts leaving an audio message saying where we've gone and asking our neighbors Riley or Maurice, whoever arrives first, to finish preparing the refreshments and entertain everyone until we return. It's almost a two-hour drive from one side of the mountains to the other, plus forty minutes beforehand to reach the first pass, though I'd bet Dad's about to do it in thirty. We're going to be late getting back.

My hand trembles slightly as I lift my rifle from the rack and head outside, Father Benedict's bright eyes and cheerful laugh filling my mind.

Lord, please let us be in time.

Get
A VERY JURASSIC CHRISTMAS
from your favorite retailer today!

ABOUT THE AUTHOR

Corinna Turner has been writing since she was fourteen and likes strong protagonists with plenty of integrity. Although she spends as much time as possible writing, she cannot keep up with the flow of ideas, for which she offers thanks—and occasional grumbles!—to the Holy Spirit. She is the author of over twenty-five books, including the Carnegie Medal Nominated I Am Margaret series, and her work has been translated into four languages. She was awarded the St. Katherine Drexel award in 2022.

She is a Lay Dominican with an MA in English from Oxford University and lives in the UK. She is a member of a number of organizations, including the Society of Authors, the Catholic Writers Guild, Catholic Teen Books, Catholic Reads, the Angelic Warfare Confraternity, and the Sodality of the Blessed Sacrament. She used to have a Giant African Land Snail, Peter, with a 6½" long shell, but now makes do with a cactus and a campervan.

Get in touch with Corinna...

Facebook: Corinna Turner

Twitter: @CorinnaTAuthor